W9-BVD-546

FROM THE
LIBRARY OF:

# CHRISTMAS (🐧) CLASSICS

## *Give the gift of literature this Christmas.*

Penguin Christmas Classics honor the power of literature to keep on giving through the ages. The five volumes in the series are not only our most beloved Christmas tales, they also have given us much of what we love about the holiday itself. *A Christmas Carol* revived in Victorian England such Christmas hallmarks as the Christmas tree, holiday cards, and caroling. The Yuletide yarns of Anthony Trollope popularized throughout the British Empire and around the world the trappings of Christmas in London. The holiday tales of Louisa May Alcott shaped the ideal of an American Christmas. *The Night Before Christmas* brought forth some of our earliest Christmas traditions as passed down through folktales. And *The Nutcracker* inspired the most famous ballet in history, one seen by millions in the twilight of every year.

Beautifully designed—with foil-stamped jackets, decorative endpapers, and nameplates for personalization—and printed in a small trim size that makes them perfect stocking stuffers, Penguin Christmas Classics embody the spirit of giving that is at the heart of our most time-honored stories about the holiday.

### Collect all five Penguin Christmas Classics:

*A Christmas Carol* by Charles Dickens

*Christmas at Thompson Hall: And Other Christmas Stories*
by Anthony Trollope

*A Merry Christmas: And Other Christmas Stories*
by Louisa May Alcott

*The Night Before Christmas* by Nikolai Gogol

*The Nutcracker* by E. T. A. Hoffmann

## CHRISTMAS AT THOMPSON HALL

*Christmas at Thompson Hall* brings together the best of the Christmas stories of Anthony Trollope, one of the most successful, prolific, and respected English novelists of the nineteenth century. Characterized by insightful, psychologically rich, and sometimes wryly humorous depictions of the middle class and gentry of Victorian England—and inspired occasionally by missives in the "lost letter" box of the provincial post office that Trollope ran—these tales helped to enshrine the traditions of the decorated Christmas tree, the holiday turkey, and the giving of store-bought gifts. Today, they open a window onto a time when carolers filled the streets and each house's door displayed a wreath of evergreen boughs, a time at once distant and yet startlingly familiar.

PENGUIN ⟨🐧⟩ CLASSICS

## CHRISTMAS AT THOMPSON HALL

**Anthony Trollope** (1815–82) was born in London. His father was a barrister who went bankrupt; the family was maintained by his mother, Frances, who resourcefully in later life became a bestselling writer. Trollope's education was disjointed, and his childhood generally seems to have been an unhappy one. Trollope enjoyed considerable acclaim as a novelist during his lifetime, publishing more than forty novels and many short stories, at the same time following a notable career as a civil servant in the British Postal Service. *The Warden* (1855), the first of his novels to achieve success, was followed by the sequence of "Barsetshire" novels, *Barchester Towers* (1857), *Doctor Thorne* (1858), *Framley Parsonage* (1861), *The Small House at Allington* (1864), and *The Last Chronicle of Barset* (1867). This series, regarded by some as his masterpiece, demonstrates Trollope's imaginative grasp of the great preoccupation of eighteenth- and nineteenth-century English novels—property—and features a gallery of recurring characters, among them the worldly cleric, Archdeacon Grantly; the immortal Mrs. Proudie; and the saintly warden, Septimus Harding. Almost equally popular were Trollope's six Palliser novels, comprising *Can You Forgive Her?* (1865), *Phineas Finn* (1869), *The Eustace Diamonds* (1873), *Phineas Redux* (1874), *The Prime Minister* (1876), and *The Duke's Children* (1880). Among his other novels are *He Knew He Was Right* (1869) and *The Way We Live Now* (1875), each regarded by some as among the greatest of nineteeth-century fiction.

# Christmas at Thompson Hall

## AND OTHER CHRISTMAS STORIES

*A*NTHONY
*T*ROLLOPE

PENGUIN BOOKS

**PENGUIN BOOKS**

Published by the Penguin Group

Penguin Group (USA) LLC

375 Hudson Street

New York, New York 10014

USA | Canada | UK | Ireland | Australia
New Zealand | India | South Africa | China
penguin.com
A Penguin Random House Company

This edition published in Penguin Books 2014

Penguin supports copyright. Copyright fuels creativity,
encourages diverse voices, promotes free speech, and creates a
vibrant culture. Thank you for buying an authorized edition of
this book and for complying with copyright laws by not
reproducing, scanning, or distributing any part of it in any form
without permission. You are supporting writers and allowing
Penguin to continue to publish books for every reader.

LIBRARY OF CONGRESS CATALOGING-IN-PUBLICATION DATA

Trollope, Anthony, 1815–1882.

[Short stories. Selections]

Christmas at Thompson Hall, and other Christmas stories / Anthony Trollope.

pages cm—(Penguin classics)

ISBN 978-0-14-312247-0 (hc.)

1. Christmas stories, English.   I. Title.

PR5682 2014

823'.8—dc23

2014012090

Printed in the United States of America

1  3  5  7  9  10  8  6  4  2

Set in LTC Cloister and Photoplay ITC

Designed by Sabrina Bowers

# Contents

# Christmas at Thompson Hall

# Christmas at Thompson Hall

## MRS. BROWN'S SUCCESS

Everyone remembers the severity of the Christmas of 187-. I will not designate the year more closely, lest I should enable those who are too curious to investigate the circumstances of this story, and inquire into details which I do not intend to make known. That winter, however, was especially severe, and the cold of the last ten days of December was more felt, I think, in Paris than in any part of England. It may, indeed, be doubted whether there is any town in any country in which thoroughly bad weather is more afflicting than in the French capital. Snow and hail seem to be colder there, and fires certainly are less warm, than in London. And then there is a feeling among visitors to Paris that Paris ought to be gay; that gaiety, prettiness, and liveliness are its aims, as money, commerce, and general business are the aims of

London, — which with its outside sombre darkness does often seem to want an excuse for its ugliness. But on this occasion, at this Christmas of 187-, Paris was neither gay nor pretty nor lively. You could not walk the streets without being ankle deep, not in snow, but in snow that had just become slush; and there were falling throughout the day and night of the 23rd of December a succession of damp half-frozen abominations from the sky which made it almost impossible for men and women to go about their business.

It was at ten o'clock on that evening that an English lady and gentleman arrived at the Grand Hotel on the Boulevard des Italiens. As I have reasons for concealing the names of this married couple I will call them Mr. and Mrs. Brown. Now I wish it to be understood that in all the general affairs of life this gentleman and this lady lived happily together, with all the amenities which should bind a husband and a wife. Mrs. Brown was one of a wealthy family, and Mr. Brown, when he married her, had been relieved from the necessity of earning his bread. Nevertheless she had at once yielded to him when he expressed a desire to spend the winters of their life in the South of France; and he, though he was by disposition somewhat idle, and but little prone to the energetic occupations of life, would generally allow himself, at other periods of the year, to be carried hither and thither by her, whose more robust nature delighted in the excitement of travelling. But on this occasion there had been a little difference between them.

Early in December an intimation had reached Mrs. Brown at Pau that on the coming Christmas there was to be a great gathering of all the Thompsons in the Thompson family hall at Stratford-le-Bow, and that she who had been a Thompson was desired to join the party with her husband. On this occasion her only sister was desirous of introducing to the family generally a most excellent young man to whom she had recently become engaged. The Thompsons, — the real name, however, is in fact concealed, — were a numerous and a thriving people. There were uncles and cousins and brothers who had all done well in the world, and who were all likely to do better still. One had lately been returned to Parliament for the Essex Flats, and was at the time of which I am writing a conspicuous member of the gallant Conservative majority. It was partly in triumph at this success that the great Christmas gathering of the Thompsons was to be held, and an opinion had been expressed by the legislator himself that should Mrs. Brown, with her husband, fail to join the family on this happy occasion she and he would be regarded as being *fainéant* Thompsons.

Since her marriage, which was an affair now nearly eight years old, Mrs. Brown had never passed a Christmas in England. The desirability of doing so had often been mooted by her. Her very soul craved the festivities of holly and min-cepies. There had ever been meetings of the Thompsons at Thompson Hall, though meetings not so significant, not so important to the family, as this one which was now to be collected. More than once had she expressed a wish to see old Christmas again in the old house among the old faces. But her husband had always pleaded a certain weakness about his throat and chest as a reason for remaining among the delights of Pau. Year after year she had yielded; and now this loud summons had come.

It was not without considerable trouble that she had induced Mr. Brown to come as far as Paris. Most unwillingly had he left Pau; and then, twice on his journey, — both at Bordeaux and Tours, — he had made an attempt to return. From the first moment he had pleaded his throat, and when at last he had consented to make the journey he had stipulated for sleeping at those two towns and at Paris. Mrs. Brown, who, without the slightest feeling of fatigue, could have made the journey from Pau to Stratford without stopping, had assented to everything, — so that they might be at Thompson Hall on Christmas Eve. When Mr. Brown uttered his unavailing complaints at the two first towns at which they stayed, she did not perhaps quite believe all that he said of his own condition. We know how prone the strong are to suspect the weakness of the weak, — as the weak are to

be disgusted by the strength of the strong. There were perhaps a few words between them on the journey, but the result
had hitherto been in favour of the lady. She had succeeded
in bringing Mr. Brown as far as Paris.

Had the occasion been less important, no doubt she
would have yielded. The weather had been bad even when
they left Pau, but as they had made their way northwards it
had become worse and still worse. As they left Tours Mr.
Brown, in a hoarse whisper, had declared his conviction that
the journey would kill him. Mrs. Brown, however, had unfortunately noticed half an hour before that he had scolded
the waiter on the score of an overcharged franc or two with a
loud and clear voice. Had she really believed that there was
danger, or even suffering, she would have yielded; — but no
woman is satisfied in such a matter to be taken in by false
pretences. She observed that he ate a good dinner on his way
to Paris, and that he took a small glass of cognac with com-
plete relish, — which a man really suffering from bronchitis
surely would not do. So she persevered, and brought him
into Paris, late in the evening, in the midst of all that slush
and snow. Then, as they sat down to supper, she thought
that he did speak hoarsely, and her loving feminine heart
began to misgive her.

But this now was at any rate clear to her, — that he could
not be worse off by going on to London than he would be

should he remain in Paris. If a man is to be ill he had better be ill in the bosom of his family than at a hotel. What comfort could he have, what relief, in that huge barrack? As for the cruelty of the weather, London could not be worse than Paris, and then she thought she had heard that sea air is good for a sore throat. In that bedroom which had been allotted to them *au quatrième*, they could not even get a decent fire. It would in every way be wrong now to forego the great Christmas gathering when nothing could be gained by staying in Paris.

She had perceived that as her husband became really ill he became also more tractable and less disputatious. Immediately after that little glass of cognac he had declared that he would be —————— if he would go beyond Paris, and she began to fear that, after all, everything would have been done in vain. But as they went down to supper between ten and eleven he was more subdued, and merely remarked that this journey would, he was sure, be the death of him. It was half-past eleven when they got back to their bedroom, and then he seemed to speak with good sense, — and also with much real apprehension. "If I can't get something to relieve me I know I shall never make my way on," he said. It was intended that they should leave the hotel at half-past five the next morning, so as to arrive at Stratford, travelling by the tidal train, at half-past seven on Christmas Eve. The early hour, the long journey, the infamous weather, the prospect of that horrid gulf between Boulogne and Folkestone, would have been as nothing to Mrs. Brown, had it not been for that settled look of anguish which had now pervaded her husband's face. "If you don't find something to relieve me I shall never live through it," he said again, sinking back into the questionable comfort of a Parisian hotel arm-chair.

"But, my dear, what can I do?" she asked, almost in tears, standing over him and caressing him. He was a thin, genteel-looking man, with a fine long, soft brown beard, a little bald at the top of the head, but certainly a genteel-looking man. She loved him dearly, and in her softer moods was apt to spoil him with her caresses. "What can I do, my dearie? You know I would do anything if I could. Get into bed, my pet, and be warm, and then to-morrow morning you will be all right." At this moment he was preparing himself for his bed, and she was assisting him. Then she tied a piece of flannel round his throat, and kissed him, and put him in beneath the bedclothes.

"I'll tell you what you can do," he said very hoarsely. His voice was so bad now that she could hardly hear him. So she crept close to him, and bent over him. She would do anything if he would only say what. Then he told her what was his plan. Down in the salon he had seen a large jar of mustard standing on a sideboard. As he left the room he had

7

observed that this had not been withdrawn with the other appurtenances of the meal. If she could manage to find her way down there, taking with her a handkerchief folded for the purpose, and if she could then appropriate a part of the contents of that jar, and returning with her prize, apply it to his throat, he thought that he could get some relief, so that he might be able to leave his bed the next morning at five. "But I am afraid it will be very disagreeable for you to go down all alone at this time of night," he croaked out in a piteous whisper.

"Of course I'll go," said she. "I don't mind going in the least. Nobody will bite me," and she at once began to fold a clean handkerchief. "I won't be two minutes, my darling, and if there is a grain of mustard in the house I'll have it on your chest almost immediately." She was a woman not easily cowed, and the journey down into the salon was nothing to her. Before she went she tucked the clothes carefully up to his ears, and then she started.

To run along the first corridor till she came to a flight of stairs was easy enough, and easy enough to descend them. Then there was another corridor, and another flight, and a third corridor and a third flight, and she began to think that she was wrong. She found herself in a part of the hotel which she had not hitherto visited, and soon discovered by looking through an open door or two that she had found her way among a set of private sitting-rooms which she had not seen before. Then she tried to make her way back, up the same stairs and through the same passages, so that she might start again. She was beginning to think that she had lost herself altogether, and that she would be able to find neither the salon nor her bedroom, when she happily met the night-porter. She was dressed in a loose white dressing-gown, with a white net over her loose hair, and with white worsted slippers. I ought perhaps to have described her personal appearance sooner. She was a large woman, with a commanding bust, thought by some to be handsome, after the manner of Juno. But with strangers there was a certain severity of manner about her, — a fortification, as it were, of her virtue against all possible attacks, — a declared determination to maintain at all points, the beautiful character of a British matron, which, much as it had been appreciated at Thompson Hall, had met with some ill-natured criticism among French men and women. At Pau she had been called La Fière Anglaise. The name had reached her own ears and those of her husband. He had been much annoyed, but she had taken it in good part, — and had endeavoured to live up to it. With her husband she could, on occasion, be soft, but she was of the opinion that with other men a British matron should be stern. She was now greatly in want of assistance; but, nevertheless, when she met the porter she remembered still patient, and, as the man was stooping to his work, her eye was on the mustard pot. There it was, capable of containing enough to blister the throats of a score of sufferers. She edged off a little towards it while the man was busy, trying to persuade herself that he would surely forgive her if she took the mustard, and told him her whole story. But the descent from her Juno bearing would have been so great! She must have owned, not only to the quest for mustard, but also to a fib, — and she could not do it. The porter was at last of the opinion that Madame must have made a mistake, and Madame acknowledged that she was afraid it was so.

With a longing, lingering eye, with an eye turned back, oh! so sadly, to the great jar, she left the room, the porter leading the way. She assured him that she would find it by herself, but he would not leave her till he had put her on to the proper passage. The journey seemed to be longer now even than before, but as she ascended the many stairs she swore to herself that she would not even yet be baulked of her object. Should her husband want comfort for his poor throat, and the comfort be there within her reach, and he not have it? She counted every stair as she went up, and marked every turn well. She was sure now that she would know the way, and that she could return to the room without fault. She would go back to the salon. Even though the man should encounter her again, she would go boldly forward and been explained so easily at first would now be as difficult of explanation. At last she was in the great public vestibule, which she was now visiting for the third time, and of which, at her last visit, she had taken the bearings accurately. The door was there — closed, indeed, but it opened easily to the hand. In the hall, and on the stairs, and along the passages, there had been gas, but here there was no light beyond that given by the little taper which she carried. When accompanied by the porter she had not feared the darkness, but now there was something in the obscurity which made her dread to walk the length of the room up to the mustard jar. She paused, and listened, and trembled. Then she thought of the glories of Thompson Hall, of the genial warmth of a British Christmas, of that proud legislator who was her first cousin, and with a rush she made good the distance, and laid her hand upon the copious delft. She looked round, but there was no one there; no sound was heard; not the distant creak of a shoe, not a rattle from one of those doors. As she paused with her fair hand upon the top of the jar, while the other held the white cloth on which the medicinal compound was to be placed, she looked like Lady Macbeth as she listened at Duncan's chamber door.

There was no doubt as to the sufficiency of the contents. The jar was full nearly up to the lips. The mixture was, no doubt, very different from that good wholesome English mustard which your cook makes fresh for you, with a little water, in two minutes. It was impregnated with a sour odour, and was, to English eyes, unwholesome of colour. But still it was mustard. She seized the horn spoon, and without further delay spread an ample sufficiency on the folded square of the handkerchief. Then she commenced to hurry her return.

But still there was a difficulty, no thought of which had occurred to her before. The candle occupied one hand, so that she had but the other for the sustenance of her treasure. Had she brought a plate or saucer from the salon, it would have been all well. As it was she was obliged to keep her eye intent on her right hand, and to proceed very slowly on her return journey. She was surprised to find what an aptitude the thing had to slip from her grasp. But still she progressed slowly, and was careful not to miss a turning. At last she was safe at her chamber door. There it was, No. 333.

## MRS. BROWN'S FAILURE

With her eye still fixed upon her burden, she glanced up at the number of the door — 333. She had been determined all through not to forget that. Then she turned the latch and crept in. The chamber also was dark after the gaslight on the stairs, but that was so much the better. She herself had put out the two candles on the dressing-table before she had left her husband. As she was closing the door behind her she paused, and could hear that he was sleeping. She was well aware that she had been long absent, — quite long enough for a man to fall into slumber who was given that way. She must have been gone, she thought, fully an hour. There had been no end to that turning over of napkins which she had so well known to be altogether vain. She paused at the centre table of the room, still looking at the mustard, which she now delicately dried from off her hand. She had had no idea that it would have been so difficult to carry so light and so small an affair. But there it was, and nothing had been lost. She took some small instrument from the washing-stand, and with the handle collected the flowing fragments into the centre. Then the question occurred to her whether, as her husband was sleeping so sweetly, it would be well to disturb him. She listened again, and felt that the slight murmur of a snore with which her ears were regaled was altogether free from any real malady in the throat. Then it occurred to her, that after all, fatigue perhaps had only made him cross. She bethought herself how, during the whole journey, she had failed to believe in his illness. What meals he had eaten! How thoroughly he had been able to enjoy his full complement of cigars! And then that glass of brandy, against which bedside. Even though he was behaving badly to her, she would not cause him discomfort by waking him roughly. She would do a wife's duty to him as a British matron should. She would not only put the warm mixture on his neck, but would sit carefully by him for twenty minutes, so that she might relieve him from it when the proper period should have come for removing the counter irritation from his throat. There would doubtless be some little difficulty in this, — in collecting the mustard after it had served her purpose. Had she been at home, surrounded by her own comforts, the application would have been made with some delicate linen bag, through which the pungency of the spice would have penetrated with strength sufficient for the purpose. But the circumstance of the occasion had not admitted this. She had, she felt, done wonders in achieving so much success as this which she had obtained. If there should be anything disagreeable in the operation he must submit to it. He had asked for mustard for his throat, and mustard he should have.

As these thoughts passed quickly through her mind, leaning over him in the dark, with her eye fixed on the mixture lest it should slip, she gently raised his flowing beard with her left hand, and with her other inverted rapidly, steadily but very softly fixed the handkerchief on his throat. From the bottom of his chin to the spot at which the collar bones meeting together form the orifice of the chest it covered the whole noble expanse. There was barely time for a glance, but never had she been more conscious of the grand proportions of that manly throat. A sweet feeling of pity came upon her, causing her to determine to relieve his sufferings in the shorter space of fifteen minutes. He had been lying on his back, with his lips apart, and as she held back his beard, that and her hand nearly covered the features of his face. But he made no violent effort to free himself from the encounter. He did not even move an arm or a leg. He simply emitted a snore louder than any that had come before. She was aware that it was not his wont to be so loud — that there was generally something more delicate and perhaps more querulous in his nocturnal voice, but then the present circumstances were exceptional. She dropped the beard very softly — and there on the pillow before her lay the face of a stranger. She had put the mustard plaster on the wrong man.

Not Priam wakened in the dead of night, not Dido when first she learned that Æneas had fled, not Othello when he learned that Desdemona had been chaste, not Medea when she became conscious of her slaughtered children, could have been more struck with horror than was this British matron as she stood for a moment gazing with awe on that stranger's bed. One vain, half-completed, snatching grasp she made at the handkerchief, and then drew back her hand. If she were

to touch him would he not wake at once, and find her standing there in his bedroom? And then how could she explain it?
By what words could she so quickly make him know the circumstances of that strange occurrence that he should accept it
all before he had said a word that might offend her? For a moment she stood all but paralysed after that faint ineffectual
movement of her arm. Then he stirred his head uneasily on
the pillow, opened wider his lips, and twice in rapid succession
snored louder than before. She started back a couple of paces,
and with her body placed between him and the candle, with
her face averted, but with her hand still resting on the foot of
the bed, she endeavoured to think what duty required of her.

She had injured the man. Though she had done it most
unwittingly, there could be no doubt but that she had injured
him. If for a moment she could be brave, the injury might in
truth be little; but how disastrous might be the consequences
if she were now in her cowardice to leave him, who could tell?
Applied for fifteen or twenty minutes a mustard plaster may
be the salvation of a throat ill at ease, but if left there
throughout the night upon the neck of a strong man, ailing
nothing, only too prone in his strength to slumber soundly,
how sad, how painful, for aught she knew how dangerous
might be the effects! And surely it was an error which any
man with a heart in his bosom would pardon! Judging from
what little she had seen of him she thought that he must

tell the story and would bid him to find the necessary aid. Alas! as she told herself that she would do so, she knew well that she was only running from the danger which it was her duty to encounter. Once again she put out her hand as though to return along the bed. Then thrice he snorted louder than before, and moved up his knee uneasily beneath the clothes as though the sharpness of the mustard were already working upon his skin. She watched him for a moment longer, and then, with the candle in her hand, she fled.

Poor human nature! Had he been an old man, even a middle-aged man, she would not have left him to his unmerited sufferings. As it was, though she completely recognised her duty, and knew what justice and goodness demanded of her, she could not do it. But there was still left to her that plan of sending the night-porter to him. It was not till she was out of the room and had gently closed the door behind her, that she began to bethink herself how she had made the mistake. With a glance of her eye she looked up, and then saw the number on the door: 353. Remarking to herself, with a Briton's natural criticism on things French, that those horrid foreigners do not know how to make their figures, she scudded rather than ran along the corridor, and then down some stairs and along another passage, — so that she might not be found in the neighbourhood should the poor man in his agony rush rapidly from his bed.

In the confusion of her first escape she hardly ventured to look for her own passage, — nor did she in the least know how she had lost her way when she came upstairs with the mustard in her hand. But at the present moment her chief object was the night-porter. She went on descending till she came again to that vestibule, and looking up at the clock saw that it was now past one. It was not yet midnight when she left her husband, but she was not at all astonished at the lapse of time. It seemed to her as though she had passed a night among these miseries. And, oh, what a night! But there was yet much to be done. She must find that porter, and then return to her own suffering husband. Ah, — what now should she say to him! If he should really be ill, how should she assuage him? And yet how more than ever necessary was it that they should leave that hotel early in the morning, — that they should leave Paris by the very earliest and quickest train that would take them as fugitives from their present dangers! The door of the salon was open, but she had no courage to go in search of a second supply. She would have lacked strength to carry it up the stairs. Where now, oh, where, was that man? From the vestibule she made her way into the hall, but everything seemed to be deserted. Through the glass she could see a light in the court beyond, but she could not bring herself to endeavour even to open the hall doors.

And now she was very cold, — chilled to her very bones. All this had been done at Christmas, and during such severity of weather as had never before been experienced by living Parisians. A feeling of great pity for herself gradually came upon her. What wrong had she done that she should be so grievously punished? Why should she be driven to wander about in this way till her limbs were failing her? And then, so absolutely important as it was that her strength should support her in the morning! The man would not die even though he were left there without aid, to rid himself of the cataplasm as best he might. Was it absolutely necessary that she should disgrace herself?

But she could not even procure the means of disgracing herself, if that telling her story to the night-porter would have been, a disgrace. She did not find him, and at last resolved to make her way back to her own room without further quest. She began to think that she had done all that she could do. No man was ever killed by a mustard plaster on his throat. His discomfort at the worst would not be worse than hers had been — or too probably than that of her poor husband. So she went back up the stairs and along the passages, and made her way on this occasion to the door of her room without any difficulty. The way was so well known to her that she could not but wonder that she had failed before. But now her hands had been empty, and her eyes had been at her full command. She looked up, and there was the number, very manifest on this occasion, — 333. She opened the door most gently, thinking that her husband might be sleeping as soundly as that other man had slept, and she crept into the room.

## MRS. BROWN ATTEMPTS TO ESCAPE

But her husband was not sleeping. He was not even in bed, as she had left him. She found him sitting there before the fireplace, on which one half-burned log still retained a spark of what had once pretended to be a fire. Nothing more wretched than his appearance could be imagined. There was a single lighted candle on the table, on which he was leaning with his two elbows, while his head rested between his hands. He had on a dressing-gown over his night-shirt, but otherwise was not clothed. He shivered audibly, or rather shook himself with the cold, and made the table to chatter as she entered the room. Then he groaned, and let his head fall from his hands on to the table. It occurred to her at the moment as she recognised the tone of his querulous voice, and as she saw the form of his neck, that she must have been deaf and blind when she had mistaken that stalwart stranger for her husband. "Oh, my dear," she said, "why are you not in bed?" He answered nothing in words, but only groaned again. "Why did you get up? I left you warm and comfortable."

"Where have you been all night?" he half whispered, half croaked, with an agonising effort.

"I have been looking for the mustard."

"Have been looking all night and haven't found it? Where have you been?"

She refused to speak a word to him till she had got him into bed, and then she told her story. But, alas, that which she told was not the true story! As she was persuading him to go back to his rest, and while she arranged the clothes again around him, she with difficulty made up her mind as to what she would do and what she would say. Living or dying he must be made to start for Thompson Hall at half-past five on the next morning. It was no longer a question of the amenities of Christmas, no longer a mere desire to satisfy the family ambition of her own people, no longer an anxiety to see her new brother-in-law. She was conscious that there was in that house one whom she had deeply injured, and from whose vengeance, even from whose aspect, she must fly. How could she endure to see that face which she was so well sure that she would recognise, or to hear the slightest sound of that voice which would be quite familiar to her ears, though it had never spoken a word in her hearing? She must certainly fly on the wings of the earliest train which would carry her towards the old house; but in order that she might do so she must propitiate her husband.

So she told her story. She had gone forth, as he had bade her, in search of the mustard, and then had suddenly lost her way. Up and down the house she had wandered, perhaps nearly a dozen times. "Had she met no one?" he asked in that raspy, husky whisper. "Surely there must have been some one about the hotel! Nor was it possible that she could have been roaming about all those hours." "Only one hour, my dear," she said. Then there was a question about the duration of time, in which both of them waxed angry, and as she became angry her husband waxed stronger, and as he became violent beneath the clothes the comfortable idea returned to her that he was not perhaps so ill as he would seem to be. She found herself driven to tell him something about the porter, having to account for that lapse of time by explaining how she had driven the poor man to search for the handkerchief which she had never lost.

"Why did you not tell him you wanted the mustard?"

"My dear!"

"Why not? There is nothing to be ashamed of in wanting mustard."

"At one o'clock in the morning! I couldn't do it. To tell you the truth, he wasn't very civil, and I thought that he was, — perhaps a little tipsy. Now, my dear, do go to sleep."

"Why didn't you get the mustard?"

"There was none there, — nowhere at all about the room. I went down again and searched everywhere. That's what took me so long. They always lock up those kind of things at these French hotels. They are too close-fisted to leave anything out. When you first spoke of it I knew that it would be gone when I got there. Now, my dear, do go to sleep, because we positively must start in the morning."

"That is impossible," said he, jumping up in the bed.

"We must go, my dear. I say that we must go. After all that has passed I wouldn't not be with Uncle John and my cousin Robert to-morrow evening for more, — more, — more than I would venture to say."

"Bother!" he exclaimed.

"It's all very well for you to say that, Charles, but you don't know. I say that we must go to-morrow, and we will."

"I do believe you want to kill me, Mary."

"That is very cruel, Charles, and most false, and most unjust. As for making you ill, nothing could be so bad for you as this wretched place, where nobody can get warm either day or night. If anything will cure your throat for you at once it will be the sea air. And only think how much more comfortable they can make you at Thompson Hall than anywhere in this country. I have so set my heart upon it, Charles, that I will do it. If we are not there to-morrow night Uncle John won't consider us as belonging to the family."

"I don't believe a word of it."

"Jane told me so in her letter. I wouldn't let you know before because I thought it so unjust. But that has been the reason why I've been so earnest about it all through."

It was a thousand pities that so good a woman should have been driven by the sad stress of circumstances to tell so many fibs. One after another she was compelled to invent them, that there might be a way open to her of escaping the horrors of a prolonged sojourn in that hotel. At length, after much grumbling, he became silent, and she trusted that he was sleeping. He had not as yet said that he would start at the required hour in the morning, but she was perfectly determined in her own mind that he should be made to do so. As he lay there motionless, and as she wandered about the room pretending to pack her things, she more than once almost resolved that she would tell him everything. Surely then he would be ready to make any effort. But there came upon her an idea that he might perhaps fail to see all the circumstances, and that, so failing, he would insist on remaining that he might tender some apology to the injured gentleman. An apology might have been very well had she not left him there in his misery — but what apology would be possible now? She would have to see him and speak to him, and everyone in the hotel would know every detail of the story. Everyone in France would know that it was she who had gone to the strange man's bedside, and put the mustard plaster on the strange man's throat in the dead of night! She could not tell the story even to her husband, lest even her husband should betray her.

Her own sufferings at the present moment were not light. In her perturbation of mind she had foolishly resolved that she would not herself go to bed. The tragedy of the night had seemed to her too deep for personal comfort. And then how would it be were she to sleep, and have no one to call her? It was imperative that she should have all her powers ready for thoroughly arousing him. It occurred to her that the servant of the hotel would certainly run her too short of time. She had to work for herself and for him too, and therefore she would not sleep. But she was very cold, and she put on first a shawl over her dressing-gown and then a cloak. She could not consume all the remaining hours of the night in packing one bag and one portmanteau, so that at last she sat down on the narrow red cotton velvet sofa, and, looking at her watch, perceived that as yet it was not much past two o'clock. How was she to get through those other three long, tedious, chilly hours?

Then there came a voice from the bed — "Ain't you coming?"

"I hoped you were asleep, my dear."

"I haven't been asleep at all. You'd better come, if you don't mean to make yourself as ill as I am."

"You are not so very bad, are you, darling?"

"I don't know what you call bad. I never felt my throat so choked in my life before!" Still as she listened she thought that she remembered his throat to have been more choked. If the husband of her bosom could play with her feelings and deceive her on such an occasion as this, — then, then, — then she thought that she would rather not have any husband of her bosom at all. But she did creep into bed, and lay down beside him without saying another word.

Of course she slept, but her sleep was not the sleep of the blest. At every striking of the clock in the quadrangle she would start up in alarm, fearing that she had let the time go by. Though the night was so short it was very long to her. But he slept like an infant. She could hear from his breathing that he was not quite so well as she could wish him to be, but still he was resting in beautiful tranquility. Not once did he move when she started up, as she did so frequently. Orders had been given and repeated over and over again that they should be called at five. The man in the office had almost been angry as he assured Mrs. Brown for the fourth time that Monsieur and Madame would most assuredly be wakened at the appointed time. But still she would trust no one, and was up and about the room before the clock had struck half-past four.

In her heart of hearts she was very tender towards her husband. Now, in order that he might feel a gleam of warmth while he was dressing himself, she collected together the fragments of half-burned wood, and endeavoured to make a little fire. Then she took out from her bag a small pot, and a patent lamp, and some chocolate, and prepared for him a warm drink, so that he might have it instantly as he was awakened. She would do anything for him in the way of ministering to his comfort — only he must go! Yes, he certainly must go!

And then she wondered how that strange man was bearing himself at the present moment. She would fain have ministered to him too had it been possible; but ah! — it was so impossible! Probably before this he would have been aroused from his troubled slumbers. But then — how aroused? At what time in the night would the burning heat upon his chest have awakened him to a sense of torture which must have been so altogether incomprehensible to him? Her strong imagination showed to her a clear picture of the scene, — clear, though it must have been done in the dark. How he must have tossed and hurled himself under the clothes; how those strong knees must have worked themselves up and down before the potent god of sleep would allow him to return to perfect consciousness; how his fingers, restrained by no reason, would have trampled over his feverish throat, scattering everywhere that unhappy poultice! Then when he should have sat up wide awake, but still in the dark — with her mind's eye she saw it all — feeling that some fire as from the infernal regions had fallen upon him but whence he would know not, how fiercely wild would be the working of his spirit! Ah, now she knew, now she felt, now she acknowledged how bound she had been to awaken him at the moment, whatever might have been the personal inconvenience to herself! In such a position what would he do — or rather what had he done? She could follow much of it in her own thoughts; — how he would scramble madly from his bed, and with one hand still on his throat, would snatch hurriedly at the matches with the other. How the light would come, and how then he would rush to the mirror. Ah, what a sight he would behold! She could see it all to the last widespread daub.

But she could not see, she could not tell herself, what in such a position a man would do; — at any rate, not what that man would do. Her husband, she thought, would tell his wife, and then the two of them, between them, would — put up with it. There are misfortunes which, if they be published, are simply aggravated by ridicule. But she remembered the features of the stranger as she had seen them at that instant in which she had dropped his beard, and she thought that there was a ferocity in them, a certain tenacity of self-importance, which would not permit their owner to endure such treatment in silence. Would he not storm and rage, and ring the bell, and call all Paris to witness his revenge?

But the storming and the raging had not reached her yet, and now it wanted but a quarter to five. In three-quarters of an hour they would be in that demi-omnibus which they had ordered for themselves, and in half-an-hour after that they would be flying towards Thompson Hall. Then she allowed herself to think of those coming comforts, — of those comforts so sweet, if only they would come! That very day now present to her was the 24th of December, and on that very evening she would be sitting in Christmas joy among all her uncles and cousins, holding her new brother-in-law affectionately by the hand. Oh, what a change from Pandemonium to Paradise; — from that wretched room, from that miserable house in which there was such ample cause for fear, to all the domestic Christmas bliss of the home of the Thompsons! She resolved that she would not, at any rate, be deterred by any light opposition on the part of her husband. "It wants just a quarter to five," she said, putting her hand steadily upon his shoulder, "and I'll get a cup of chocolate for you, so that you may get up comfortably."

"I've been thinking about it," he said, rubbing his eyes with the back of his hands. "It will be so much better to go over by the mail train to-night. We should be in time for Christmas just the same."

"That will not do at all," she answered, energetically. "Come, Charles, after all the trouble do not disappoint me."

"It is such a horrid grind."

"Think what I have gone through, — what I have done for you! In twelve hours we shall be there, among them all. You won't be so little like a man as not to go on now." He threw himself back upon the bed, and tried to readjust the clothes round his neck. "No, Charles, no," she continued; "not if I know it. Take your chocolate and get up. There is not a moment to be lost." With that she laid her hand upon his shoulder, and made him clearly understand that he would not be allowed to take further rest in that bed.

Grumbling, sulky, coughing continually, and declaring that life under such circumstances was not worth having, he did at last get up and dress himself. When once she saw that he was obeying her she became again tender to him, and certainly took much more than her own share of the trouble of the proceedings. Long before the time was up she was ready, and the porter had been summoned to take the luggage downstairs. When the man came she was rejoiced to see that it was not he whom she had met among the passages during her nocturnal rambles. He shouldered the box, and told them that they would find coffee and bread and butter in the small *salle-à-manger* below.

"I told you that it would be so, when you would boil that stuff," said the ungrateful man, who had nevertheless swallowed the hot chocolate when it was given to him.

They followed their luggage down into the hall; but as she went, at every step, the lady looked around her. She dreaded the sight of that porter of the night; she feared lest some potential authority of the hotel should come to her and ask her some horrid question; but of all her fears her greatest fear was that there should arise before her an apparition of that face which she had seen recumbent on its pillow.

As they passed the door of the great salon, Mr. Brown looked in. "Why, there it is still!" said he.

"What?" said she, trembling in every limb.

"The mustard pot!"

"They have put it in there since," she exclaimed energetically, in her despair. "But never mind. The omnibus is here. Come away." And she absolutely took him by the arm.

But at that moment a door behind them opened, and Mrs. Brown heard herself called by her name. And there was the night-porter, — with a handkerchief in his hand. But

ANTHONY TROLLOPE

the further doings of that morning must be told in a further chapter.


## MRS. BROWN DOES ESCAPE

It had been visible to Mrs. Brown from the first moment of her arrival on the ground floor that "something was the matter," if we may be allowed to use such a phrase; and she felt all but convinced that this something had reference to her. She fancied that the people of the hotel were looking at her as she swallowed, or tried to swallow, her coffee. When her husband was paying the bill there was something disagreeable in the eye of the man who was taking the money. Her sufferings were very great, and no one sympathised with her. Her husband was quite at his ease, except that he was complaining of the cold. When she was anxious to get him out into the carriage, he still stood there leisurely, arranging shawl after shawl around his throat. "You can do that quite as well in the omnibus," she had just said to him very crossly, when there appeared upon the scene through a side door that very porter whom she dreaded, with a soiled pocket-handkerchief in his hand.

Even before the sound of her own name met her ears Mrs. Brown knew it all. She understood the full horror of her position from that man's hostile face, and from the little article which he held in his hand. If during the watches of the night she had had money in her pocket, if she had made a friend of this greedy fellow by well-timed liberality, all might have been so different! But she reflected that she had allowed him to go unfee'd after all his trouble, and she knew that he was her enemy. It was the handkerchief that she feared. She thought that she might have brazened out anything but that. No one had seen her enter or leave that strange man's room. No one had seen her dip her hands in that jar. She had, no doubt, been found wandering about the house while the slumberer had been made to suffer so strangely, and there might have been suspicion, and perhaps accusation. But she would have been ready with frequent protestations to deny all charges made against her, and, though no one might have believed her, no one could have convicted her. Here, however, was evidence against which she would be unable to stand for a moment. At the first glance she acknowledged the potency of that damning morsel of linen.

During all the horrors of the night she had never given a thought to the handkerchief, and yet she ought to have known that the evidence it would bring against her was palpable and certain. Her name, "M. Brown," was plainly written on the corner. What a fool she had been not to have thought of this! Had she but remembered the plain marking which she, as a careful, well-conducted, British matron, had put upon all her clothes, she would at any hazard have recovered the article. Oh that she had waked the man, or bribed the porter, or even told her husband! But now she was, as it were, friendless, without support, without a word that she could say in her own defence, convicted of having committed this assault upon a strange man as he slept in his own bedroom, and then of having left him! The thing must be explained by the truth; but how to explain such truth, how to tell such story in a way to satisfy injured folk, and she with barely time sufficient to catch the train! Then it occurred to her that they could have no legal right to stop her because the pocket-handkerchief had been found in a strange gentleman's bedroom. "Yes, it is mine," she said, turning to her husband, as the porter, with a loud voice, asked if she were not Madame Brown. "Take it, Charles, and come on." Mr. Brown naturally stood still in astonishment. He did put out his hand, but the porter would not allow the evidence to pass so readily out of his custody.

"What does it all mean?" asked Mr. Brown.

"A gentleman has been — eh — eh —. Something has been done to a gentleman in his bedroom," said the clerk.

"Something done to a gentleman!" repeated Mr. Brown.

"Something very bad indeed," said the porter. "Look here," and he showed the condition of the handkerchief.

"Charles, we shall lose the train," said the affrighted wife.

"What the mischief does it all mean?" demanded the husband.

"Did Madame go into the gentleman's room?" asked the clerk. Then there was an awful silence, and all eyes were fixed upon the lady.

"What does it all mean?" demanded the husband. "Did you go into anybody's room?"

"I did," said Mrs. Brown with much dignity, looking round upon her enemies as a stag at bay will look upon the hounds which are attacking him. "Give me the handkerchief." But the night-porter quickly put it behind his back. "Charles, we cannot allow ourselves to be delayed. You shall write a letter to the keeper of the hotel, explaining it all." Then she essayed to swim out, through the front door, into the courtyard in which the vehicle was waiting for them. But three or four men and women interposed themselves, and even her husband did not seem quite ready to continue his journey. "To-night is Christmas Eve," said Mrs. Brown, "and we shall not be at Thompson Hall! Think of my sister!"

"Why did you go into the man's bedroom, my dear?" whispered Mr. Brown in English.

But the porter heard the whisper, and understood the language; — the porter who had not been "tipped." "Ye'es; — vy?" asked the porter.

"It was a mistake, Charles; there is not a moment to lose. I can explain it all to you in the carriage." Then the clerk suggested that Madame had better postpone her journey a little. The gentleman upstairs had certainly been very badly treated, and had demanded to know why so great an outrage had been perpetrated. The clerk said that he did not wish to send for the police — here Mrs. Brown gasped terribly and threw herself on her husband's shoulder, — but he did not think he could allow the party to go till the gentleman upstairs had received some satisfaction. It had now become clearly impossible that the journey could be made by the early train. Even Mrs. Brown gave it up herself, and demanded of her husband that she should be taken back to her bedroom.

"But what is to be said to the gentleman?" asked the porter.

Of course it was impossible that Mrs. Brown should be made to tell her story there in the presence of them all. The clerk, when he found he had succeeded in preventing her from leaving the house, was satisfied with a promise from Mr. Brown that he would inquire from his wife what were these mysterious circumstances, and would then come down to the office and give some explanation. If it were necessary, he would see the strange gentleman, — whom he now ascertained to be a certain Mr. Jones returning from the east of

Europe. He learned also that this Mr. Jones had been most anxious to travel by that very morning train which he and his wife had intended to use, — that Mr. Jones had been most particular in giving his orders accordingly, but that at the last moment he had declared himself to be unable even to dress himself, because of the injury which had been done him during the night. When Mr. Brown heard this from the clerk just before he was allowed to take his wife upstairs, while she was sitting on a sofa in a corner with her face hidden, a look of awful gloom came over his own countenance. What could it be that his wife had done to the gentleman of so terrible a nature? "You had better come up with me," he said to her with marital severity, and the poor cowed woman went with him tamely as might have done some patient Grizel. Not a word was spoken till they were in the room and the door was locked. "Now," said he, "what does it all mean?"

It was not till nearly two hours had passed that Mr. Brown came down the stairs very slowly, — turning it all over in his mind. He had now gradually heard the absolute and exact truth, and had very gradually learned to believe it. It was first necessary that he should understand that his wife had told him many fibs during the night; but, as she constantly alleged to him when he complained of her conduct in this respect, they had all been told on his behalf. Had she not struggled to get the mustard for his comfort, and when she had secured the prize had she not hurried to put it on, — as she had fondly thought, — his throat? And though she had fibbed to him afterwards, had she not done so in order that he might not be troubled? "You are not angry with me because I was in that man's room?" she asked, looking full into his eyes, but not quite without a sob. He paused a moment, and then declared, with something of a true husband's confidence in his tone, that he was not in the least angry with her on that account. Then she kissed him, and bade him remember that after all no one could really injure them. "What harm has been done, Charles? The gentleman won't die because he has had a mustard plaster on his throat. The worst is about Uncle John and dear Jane. They do think so much of Christmas Eve at Thompson Hall!"

Mr. Brown, when he again found himself in the clerk's office, requested that his card might be taken up to Mr. Jones. Mr. Jones had sent down his own card, which was handed to Mr. Brown: "Mr. Barnaby Jones." "And how was it all, sir?" asked the clerk, in a whisper — a whisper which had at the same time something of authoritative demand and something also of submissive respect. The clerk of course was anxious to know the mystery. It is hardly too much to say that everyone in that vast hotel was by this time anxious to have the mystery unravelled. But Mr. Brown would tell nothing to any one. "It is merely a matter to be explained between me and Mr. Jones," he said. The card was taken upstairs, and after a while he was ushered into Mr. Jones' room. It was, of course, that very 353 with which the reader is already acquainted. There was a fire burning, and the remains of Mr. Jones' breakfast were on the table. He was sitting in his dressing-gown and slippers, with his shirt open in the front, and a silk handkerchief very loosely covering his throat. Mr. Brown, as he entered the room, of course looked with considerable anxiety at the gentleman of whose condition he had heard so sad an account; but he could only observe some considerable stiffness of movement and demeanour as Mr. Jones turned his head round to greet him.

"This has been a very disagreeable accident, Mr. Jones," said the husband of the lady.

"Accident! I don't know how it could have been an accident. It has been a most — most — most — a most monstrous, — er, — er, — I must say, interference with a gentleman's privacy, and personal comfort."

"Quite so, Mr. Jones, but, — on the part of the lady, who is my wife —— "

"So I understand. I myself am about to become a married man, and I can understand what your feelings must be. I wish to say as little as possible to harrow them." Here Mr. Brown bowed. "But, — there's the fact. She did do it."

"She thought it was — me!"

"What!"

"I give you my word as a gentleman, Mr. Jones. When she was putting that mess upon you she thought it was me! She did, indeed."

Mr. Jones looked at his new acquaintance and shook his head. He did not think it possible that any woman would make such a mistake as that.

"I had a very bad sore throat," continued Mr. Brown, "and indeed you may perceive it still," — in saying this, he perhaps aggravated a little sign of his distemper, "and I asked Mrs. Brown to go down and get one, — just what she put on you."

"I wish you'd had it," said Mr. Jones, putting his hand up to his neck.

"I wish I had, — for your sake as well as mine, — and for hers, poor woman. I don't know when she will get over the shock."

"I don't know when I shall. And it has stopped me on my journey. I was to have been to-night, this very night, this Christmas Eve, with the young lady I am engaged to marry. Of course I couldn't travel. The extent of the injury done no-body can imagine at present."

"It has been just as bad to me, sir. We were to have been with our family this Christmas Eve. There were particular reasons, — most particular. We were only hindered from going by hearing of your condition."

"Why did she come into my room at all? I can't understand that. A lady always knows her own room at an hotel."

"353 — that's yours; 333 — that's ours. Don't you see how easy it was? She had lost her way, and she was a little afraid lest the thing should fall down."

"I wish it had, with all my heart."

"That's how it was. Now I'm sure, Mr. Jones, you'll take a lady's apology. It was a most unfortunate mistake, — most unfortunate; but what more can be said?"

Mr. Jones gave himself up to reflection for a few moments before he replied to this. He supposed that he was bound to believe the story as far as it went. At any rate, he did not know how he could say that he did not believe it. It seemed to him to be almost incredible, — especially incredible in regard to that personal mistake, for, except that they both had long beards and brown beards, Mr. Jones thought that there was no point of resemblance between himself and Mr. Brown. But still, even that, he felt, must be accepted. But then why had he been left, deserted, to undergo all those torments? "She found out her mistake at last, I suppose?" he said.

"Oh, yes."

"Why didn't she wake a fellow and take it off again?"

"Ah!"

"She can't have cared very much for a man's comfort when she went away and left him like that."

"Ah! there was the difficulty, Mr. Jones."

"Difficulty! Who was it that had done it? To come to me, in my bedroom, in the middle of the night and put that thing on me, and then leave it there and say nothing about it! It seems to me deuced like a practical joke."

"No, Mr. Jones!"

"That's the way I look at it," said Mr. Jones, plucking up his courage.

"There isn't a woman in all England, or in all France, less likely to do such a thing than my wife. She's as steady as a rock, Mr. Jones, and would no more go into another gentleman's bedroom in joke than —— Oh dear no! You're going to be a married man yourself."

"Unless all this makes a difference," said Mr. Jones, almost in tears. "I had sworn that I would be with her this Christmas Eve."

"Oh, Mr. Jones, I cannot believe that will interfere with your happiness. How could you think that your wife, as is to be, would do such a thing as that in joke?"

"She wouldn't do it at all; — joke or anyway."

"How can you tell what accident might happen to any one?"

46

"She'd have wakened the man then afterwards. I'm sure she would. She would never have left him to suffer in that way. Her heart is too soft. Why didn't she send you to wake me, and explain it all. That's what my Jane would have done; and I should have gone and wakened him. But the whole thing is impossible," he said, shaking his head as he remembered that he and his Jane were not in a condition as yet to undergo any such mutual trouble. At last Mr. Jones was brought to acknowledge that nothing more could be done. The lady sent her apology, and told her story, and he must bear the trouble and inconvenience to which she had subjected him. He still, however, had his own opinion about her conduct generally, and could not be brought to give any sign of amity. He simply bowed when Mr. Brown was hoping to induce him to shake hands, and sent no word of pardon to the great offender.

The matter, however, was so far concluded that there was no further question of police interference, nor any doubt but that the lady with her husband was to be allowed to leave Paris by the night train. The nature of the accident probably became known to all. Mr. Brown was interrogated by many, and though he professed to declare that he would answer no question, nevertheless he found it better to tell the clerk something of the truth than to allow the matter to be shrouded in mystery. It is to be feared that Mr. Jones, who did not once show himself through the day, but who employed the hours

and his wife to the station, but now, after his misfortunes, he contented himself with such provision as the people at the hotel might make for him. At the appointed hour he brought his wife down, thickly veiled. There were many strangers as she passed through the hall, ready to look at the lady who had done that wonderful thing in the dead of night, but none could see a feature of her face as she stepped across the hall, and was hurried into the omnibus. And there were many eyes also on Mr. Jones, who followed her very quickly, for he also, in spite of his sufferings, was leaving Paris on the evening in order that he might be with his English friends on Christmas Day. He, as he went through the crowd, assumed an air of great dignity, to which, perhaps, something was added by his endeavours, as he walked, to save his poor throat from irritation. He, too, got into the same omnibus, stumbling over the feet of his enemy in the dark. At the station they got their tickets, one close after the other, and then were brought into each other's presence in the waiting-room. I think it must be acknowledged that here Mr. Jones was conscious not only of her presence, but of her consciousness of his presence, and that he assumed an attitude, as though he should have said, "Now do you think it possible for me to believe that you mistook me for your husband?" She was perfectly quiet, but sat through that quarter of an hour with her face continually

49

veiled. Mr. Brown made some little overture of conversation to Mr. Jones, but Mr. Jones, though he did mutter some reply, showed plainly enough that he had no desire for further intercourse. Then came the accustomed stampede, the awful rush, the internecine struggle in which seats had to be found. Seats, I fancy, are regularly found, even by the most tardy, but it always appears that every British father and every British husband is actuated at these stormy moments by a conviction that unless he prove himself a very Hercules he and his daughters and his wife will be left desolate in Paris. Mr. Brown was quite Herculean, carrying two bags and a hat-box in his own hands, besides the cloaks, the coats, the rugs, the sticks, and the umbrellas. But when he had got himself and his wife well seated, with their faces to the engine, with a corner seat for her, — there was Mr. Jones immediately opposite to her. Mr. Jones, as soon as he perceived the inconvenience of his position, made a scramble for another place, but he was too late. In that contiguity the journey as far as Dover had to be made. She, poor woman, never once took up her veil. There he sat, without closing an eye, stiff as a ramrod, sometimes showing by little uneasy gestures that the trouble at his neck was still there, but never speaking a word, and hardly moving a limb.

Crossing from Calais to Dover the lady was, of course, separated from her victim. The passage was very bad, and she more than once reminded her husband how well it would have been with them now had they pursued their journey as she had intended, — as though they had been detained in Paris by his fault! Mr. Jones, as he laid himself down on his back, gave himself up to wondering whether any man before him had ever been made subject to such absolute injustice. Now and again he put his hand up to his own beard, and began to doubt whether it could have been moved, as it must have been moved, without waking him. What if chloroform had been used? Many such suspicions crossed his mind during the misery of that passage.

They were again together in the same railway carriage from Dover to London. They had now got used to the close neighbourhood, and knew how to endure each the presence of the other. But as yet Mr. Jones had never seen the lady's face. He longed to know what were the features of the woman who had been so blind — if indeed that story were true. Or if it were not true, of what like was the woman who would dare in the middle of the night to play such a trick as that. But still she kept her veil close over her face.

From Cannon Street the Browns took their departure in a cab for the Liverpool Street Station, whence they would be conveyed by the Eastern Counties Railway to Stratford. Now at any rate their troubles were over. They would be in ample time, not only for Christmas Day church, but for

ANTHONY TROLLOPE

Christmas Day breakfast. "It will be just the same as getting in there last night," said Mr. Brown, as he walked across the platform to place his wife in the carriage for Stratford. She entered it first, and as she did so there she saw Mr. Jones seated in the corner! Hitherto she had borne his presence well, but now she could not restrain herself from a little start and a little scream. He bowed his head very slightly, as though acknowledging the compliment, and then down she dropped her veil. When they arrived at Stratford, the journey being over in a quarter of an hour, Jones was out of the carriage even before the Browns.

"There is Uncle John's carriage," said Mrs. Brown, thinking that now, at any rate, she would be able to free herself from the presence of this terrible stranger. No doubt he was a handsome man to look at, but on no face so sternly hostile had she ever before fixed her eyes. She did not, perhaps, reflect that the owner of no other face had ever been so deeply injured by herself.

## MRS. BROWN AT THOMPSON HALL

"Please, sir, we were to ask for Mr. Jones," said the servant, putting his head into the carriage after both Mr. and Mrs. Brown had seated themselves.

"Mr. Jones!" exclaimed the husband.

"Why ask for Mr. Jones?" demanded the wife. The servant was about to tender some explanation when Mr. Jones stepped up and said that he was Mr. Jones. "We are going to Thompson Hall," said the lady with great vigour.

"So am I," said Mr. Jones, with much dignity. It was, however, arranged that he should sit with the coachman, as there was a rumble behind for the other servant. The luggage was put into a cart, and away all went for Thompson Hall.

"What do you think about it, Mary," whispered Mr. Brown, after a pause. He was evidently awe-struck by the horror of the occasion.

"I cannot make it out at all. What do you think?"

"I don't know what to think. Jones going to Thompson Hall!"

"He's a very good-looking young man," said Mrs. Brown.

"Well; — that's as people think. A stiff, stuck-up fellow, I should say. Up to this moment he has never forgiven you for what you did to him."

"Would you have forgiven his wife, Charles, if she'd done it to you?"

"He hasn't got a wife, — yet."

"How do you know?"

"He is coming home now to be married," said Mr. Brown. "He expects to meet the young lady this very Christmas Day. He told me so. That was one of the reasons why he was so angry at being stopped by what you did last night."

"I suppose he knows Uncle John, or he wouldn't be going to the Hall," said Mrs. Brown.

"I can't make it out," said Mr. Brown, shaking his head.

"He looks quite like a gentleman," said Mrs. Brown, "though he has been so stiff. Jones! Barnaby Jones! You're sure it was Barnaby?"

"That was the name on the card."

"Not Burnaby?" asked Mrs. Brown.

"It was Barnaby Jones on the card, — just the same as 'Barnaby Rudge,' and as for looking like a gentleman, I'm by no means quite so sure. A gentleman takes an apology when it's offered."

"Perhaps, my dear, that depends on the condition of his throat. If you had had a mustard plaster on all night, you might not have liked it. But here we are at Thompson Hall at last."

Thompson Hall was an old brick mansion, standing within a huge iron gate, with a gravel sweep before it. It had stood there before Stratford was a town, or even a suburb, and had then been known by the name Bow Place. But it had been in the hands of the present family for the last thirty years, and was now known far and wide as Thompson Hall, — a comfortable, roomy, old-fashioned place, perhaps a little dark and dull to look at, but much more substantially built than most of our modern villas. Mrs. Brown jumped with alacrity from the carriage, and with a quick step entered the home of her forefathers. Her husband followed her more leisurely, but he, too, felt that he was at home at Thompson Hall. Then Mr. Jones walked in also; — but he looked as though he were not at all at home. It was still very early, and no one of the family was as yet down. In these circumstances it was almost necessary that something should be said to Mr. Jones.

"Do you know Mr. Thompson?" asked Mr. Brown.

"I never had the pleasure of seeing him, — as yet," answered Mr. Jones, very stiffly.

"Oh, — I didn't know; — because you said you were coming here."

"And I have come here. Are you friends of Mr. Thompson?"

"Oh, dear, yes," said Mrs. Brown. "I was a Thompson myself before I married."

"Oh, — indeed!" said Mr. Jones. "How very odd; — very odd indeed."

During this time the luggage was being brought into the house, and two old family servants were offering them

assistance. Would the new comers like to go up to their bed-
rooms? Then the housekeeper, Mrs. Green, intimated with
a wink that Miss Jane would, she was sure, be down quite
immediately. The present moment, however, was still very
unpleasant. The lady probably had made her guess as to the
mystery; but the two gentlemen were still altogether in the
dark. Mrs. Brown had no doubt declared her parentage, but
Mr. Jones, with such a multitude of strange facts crowding
on his mind, had been slow to understand her. Being somewhat suspicious by nature he was beginning to think
whether possibly the mustard had been put by this lady on
his throat with some reference to his connextion with
Thompson Hall. Could it be that she, for some reason of
her own, had wished to prevent his coming, and had con-
trived this untoward stratagem out of her brain? or had she
wished to make him ridiculous to the Thompson family, —
to whom, as a family, he was at present unknown? It was
becoming more and more improbable to him that the whole
thing should have been an accident. When, after the first
horrid torments of that morning in which he had in his
agony invoked the assistance of the night-porter, he had
begun to reflect on his situation, he had determined that
it would be better that nothing further should be said
about it. What would life be worth to him if he were to
be known wherever he went as the man who had been

mustard-plastered in the middle of the night by a strange lady? The worst of a practical joke is that the remembrance of the absurd condition sticks so long to the sufferer! At the hotel that night-porter, who had possessed himself of the handkerchief and had read the name and had connected that name with the occupant of 333 whom he had found wandering about the house with some strange purpose, had not permitted the thing to sleep. The porter had pressed the matter home against the Browns, and had produced the interview which has been recorded. But during the whole of that day Mr. Jones had been resolving that he would never again either think of the Browns or speak of them. A great injury had been done to him, — a most outrageous injustice; — but it was a thing which had to be endured. A horrid woman had come across him like a nightmare. All he could do was to endeavour to forget the terrible visitation. Such had been his resolve, — in making which he had passed that long day in Paris. And now the Browns had stuck to him from the moment of his leaving his room! He had been forced to travel with them, but had travelled with them as a stranger. He had tried to comfort himself with the reflection that at every fresh stage he would shake them off. In one railway after another the vicinity had been bad, — but still they were strangers. Now he found himself in the same house with them, — where of course the story would be told. Had

piteously up into Mrs. Brown's face, as though imploring her not to tell the story.

"Perhaps, Jane, you had better introduce us," said Mrs. Brown.

"Introduce you! I thought you had been travelling together, and staying at the same hotel — and all that."

"So we have; but people may be in the same hotel without knowing each other. And we have travelled all the way home with Mr. Jones without in the least knowing who he was."

"How very odd! Do you mean you have never spoken?"

"Not a word," said Mrs. Brown.

"I do so hope you'll love each other," said Jane.

"It shan't be my fault if we don't," said Mrs. Brown.

"I'm sure it shan't be mine," said Mr. Brown, tendering his hand to the other gentleman. The various feelings of the moment were too much for Mr. Jones, and he could not respond quite as he should have done. But as he was taken upstairs to his room he determined that he would make the best of it.

The owner of the house was old Uncle John. He was a bachelor, and with him lived various members of the family. There was the great Thompson of them all, Cousin Robert, who was now member of Parliament for the Essex Flats, and young John, as a certain enterprising Thompson of the age of forty was usually called, and then there was old Aunt Bess, and among other young branches there was Miss Jane Thompson who was now engaged to marry Mr. Charles Burnaby Jones. As it happened, no other member of the family had as yet seen Mr. Burnaby Jones, and he, being by nature of a retiring disposition, felt himself to be ill at ease when he came into the breakfast-parlour among all the Thompsons. He was known to be a gentleman of good family and ample means, and all the Thompsons had approved of the match, but during that first Christmas breakfast he did not seem to accept his condition jovially. His own Jane sat beside him, but then on the other side sat Mrs. Brown. She assumed an immediate intimacy, — as women know how to do on such occasions, — being determined from the very first to regard her sister's husband as a brother; but he still feared her. She was still to him the woman who had come to him in the dead of night with that horrid mixture, — and had then left him.

"It was so odd that both of you should have been detained on the very same day," said Jane.

"Yes, it was odd," said Mrs. Brown, with a smile, looking round upon her neighbour.

"It was abominably bad weather, you know," said Brown.

"But you were both so determined to come," said the old gentleman. "When we got the two telegrams at the same moment, we were sure that there had been some agreement between you."

"Not exactly an agreement," said Mrs. Brown; whereupon Mr. Jones looked as grim as death.

"I'm sure there is something more than we understand yet," said the member of Parliament.

Then they all went to church, as a united family ought to do on Christmas Day, and came home to a fine old English early dinner at three o'clock, — a sirloin of beef a foot-and-a-half broad, a turkey as big as an ostrich, a plum-pudding bigger than the turkey, and two or three dozen mince-pies. "That's a very large bit of beef," said Mr. Jones, who had not lived much in England latterly. "It won't look so large," said the old gentleman, "when all our friends downstairs have had their say to it." "A plum-pudding on Christmas Day can't be too big," he said again, "if the cook will but take time enough over it. I never knew a bit go to waste yet."

By this time there had been some explanation as to past events between the two sisters. Mrs. Brown had indeed told Jane all about it, how ill her husband had been, how she had been forced to go down and look for the mustard, and then what she had done with the mustard. "I don't think they are a bit alike you know, Mary, if you mean that," said Jane.

"Well, no; perhaps not quite alike. I only saw his beard, you know. No doubt it was stupid, but I did it."

"Why didn't you take it off again?" asked the sister.

"Oh, Jane, if you'd only think of it? Could you!" Then of course all that occurred was explained, how they had been stopped on their journey, how Brown had made the best apology in his power, and how Jones had travelled with them and had never spoken a word. The gentleman had only taken his new name a week since but of course had had his new card printed immediately. "I'm sure I should have thought of it if they hadn't made a mistake with the first name. Charles said it was like Barnaby Rudge."

"Not at all like Barnaby Rudge," said Jane; "Charles Burnaby Jones is a very good name."

"Very good indeed, — and I'm sure that after a little bit he won't be at all the worse for the accident."

Before dinner the secret had been told no further, but still there had crept about among the Thompsons, and, indeed, downstairs also, among the retainers, a feeling that there was a secret. The old housekeeper was sure that Miss Mary, as she still called Mrs. Brown, had something to tell if she could only be induced to tell it, and that this something had reference to Mr. Jones' personal comfort. The head of the family, who was a sharp old gentleman, felt this also, and the member of Parliament, who had an idea that he specially should never be kept in the dark, was almost angry. Mr. Jones, suffering from some kindred feeling throughout the dinner, remained silent and unhappy. When two or three toasts had been drunk, — the Queen's health, the old gentleman's health, the young couple's health, Brown's health, and the general health of all the Thompsons, then tongues were loosened and a question was asked, "I know that there has been something doing in Paris between these young people that we haven't heard as yet," said the uncle. Then Mrs. Brown laughed, and Jane, laughing too, gave Mr. Jones to understand that she at any rate knew all about it.

"If there is a mystery I hope it will be told at once," said the member of Parliament, angrily.

"Come, Brown, what is it?" asked another male cousin.

"Well, there was an accident. I'd rather Jones should tell," said he.

Jones' brow became blacker than thunder, but he did not say a word. "You mustn't be angry with Mary," Jane whispered into her lover's ear.

"Come, Mary, you never were slow at talking," said the uncle.

"I do hate this kind of thing," said the member of Parliament.

"I will tell it all," said Mrs. Brown, very nearly in tears, or else pretending to be very nearly in tears. "I know I was very wrong, and I do beg his pardon, and if he won't say that he forgives me I never shall be happy again." Then she clasped her hands, and, turning round, looked him piteously in the face.

"Oh yes; I do forgive you," said Mr. Jones.

"My brother," said she, throwing her arms round him and kissing him. He recoiled from the embrace, but I think that he attempted to return the kiss. "And now I will tell the whole story," said Mrs. Brown. And she told it, acknowledging her fault with true contrition, and swearing that she would atone for it by life-long sisterly devotion.

"And you mustard-plastered the wrong man!" said the old gentleman, almost rolling off his chair with delight.

"I did," said Mrs. Brown, sobbing, "and I think that no woman ever suffered as I suffered."

"And Jones wouldn't let you leave the hotel?"

"It was the handkerchief stopped us," said Brown.

"If it had turned out to be anybody else," said the member of Parliament, "the results might have been most serious, — not to say discreditable."

"That's nonsense, Robert," said Mrs. Brown, who was disposed to resent the use of so severe a word, even from the legislator cousin.

"In a strange gentleman's bedroom!" he continued. "It only shows that what I have always said is quite true. You should never go to bed in a strange house without locking your door."

Nevertheless it was a very jovial meeting, and before the evening was over Mr. Jones was happy, and had been brought to acknowledge that the mustard plaster would probably not do him any permanent injury.

# Christmas Day
# at Kirkby Cottage

## WHAT MAURICE ARCHER SAID
## ABOUT CHRISTMAS

"After all, Christmas is a bore!"

"Even though you should think so, Mr. Archer, pray do not say so here."

"But it is."

"I am very sorry that you should feel like that; but pray do not say anything so very horrible."

"Why not? and why is it horrible? You know very well what I mean."

"I do not want to know what you mean; and it would make papa very unhappy if he were to hear you."

"A great deal of beef is roasted, and a great deal of pudding is boiled, and then people try to be jolly by eating more than usual. The consequence is, they get very sleepy, and want to go to bed an hour before the proper time. That's Christmas."

He who made this speech was a young man about twenty-three years old, and the other personage in the dialogue was a young lady, who might be, perhaps, three years his junior. The "papa" to whom the lady had alluded was the Rev. John Lownd, parson of Kirkby Cliffe, in Craven, and the scene was the parsonage library, as pleasant a little room as you would wish to see, in which the young man who thought Christmas to be a bore was at present sitting over the fire, in the parson's arm-chair, with a novel in his hand, which he had been reading till he was interrupted by the parson's daughter. It was nearly time for him to dress for dinner, and the young lady was already dressed. She had entered the room on the pretext of looking for some book or paper, but perhaps her main object may have been to ask for some assistance from Maurice Archer in the work of decorating the parish church. The necessary ivy and holly branches had been collected, and the work was to be performed on the morrow. The day following would be Christmas Day. It must be acknowledged, that Mr. Archer had not accepted the proposition made to him very graciously.

Maurice Archer was a young man as to whose future career in life many of his elder friends shook their heads and expressed much fear. It was not that his conduct was dangerously bad, or that he spent his money too fast, but that he was abominably conceited, so said these elder friends; and then there was the unfortunate fact of his being altogether beyond control. He had neither father, nor mother, nor uncle, nor guardian. He was the owner of a small property not far from Kirkby Cliffe, which gave him an income of some six or seven hundred a year, and he had altogether declined any of the professions which had been suggested to him. He had, in the course of the year now coming to a close, taken his degree at Oxford, with some academical honours, which were not high enough to confer distinction, and had already positively refused to be ordained, although, would he do so, a small living would be at his disposal on the death of a septuagenarian cousin. He intended, he said, to farm a portion of his own land, and had already begun to make amicable arrangements for buying up the interest of one of his two tenants. The rector of Kirkby Cliffe, the Rev. John Lownd, had been among his father's dearest friends, and he was now the parson's guest for Christmas.

There had been many doubts in the parsonage before the young man had been invited. Mrs. Lownd had considered that the visit would be dangerous. Their family consisted of two daughters, the youngest of whom was still a child; but Isabel was turned twenty, and if a young man were brought into the house, would it not follow, as a matter of course, that she should fall in love with him? That was the mother's first argument. "Young people don't always fall in love," said the father. "But people will say that he is brought here on purpose," said the mother, using her second argument. The parson, who in family matters generally had his own way, expressed an opinion that if they were to be governed by what other people might choose to say, their course of action would be very limited indeed. As for his girl, he did not think she would ever give her heart to any man before it had been asked; and as for the young man, — whose father had been for over thirty years his dearest friend, — if he chose to fall in love, he must run his chance, like other young men. Mr. Lownd declared he knew nothing against him, except that he was, perhaps, a little self-willed; and so Maurice Archer came to Kirkby Cliffe, intending to spend two months in the same house with Isabel Lownd.

Hitherto, as far as the parents or the neighbours saw, — and in their endeavours to see, the neighbours were very diligent, — there had been no love-making. Between Mabel, the young daughter, and Maurice, there had grown up a violent friendship, — so much so, that Mabel, who was fourteen, declared that Maurice Archer was "the jolliest person" in the world. She called him Maurice, as did Mr. and Mrs. Lownd; and to Maurice, of course, she was Mabel. But between Isabel and Maurice it was always Miss Lownd and

Mr. Archer, as was proper. It was so, at least, with this difference, that each of them had got into a way of dropping, when possible, the other's name.

It was acknowledged throughout Craven, — which my readers of course know to be a district in the northern portion of the West Riding of Yorkshire, of which Skipton is the capital, — that Isabel Lownd was a very pretty girl. There were those who thought that Mary Manniwick, of Barden, excelled her; and others, again, expressed a preference for Fanny Grange, the pink-cheeked daughter of the surgeon at Giggleswick. No attempt shall here be made to award the palm of superior merit; but it shall be asserted boldly, that no man need desire a prettier girl with whom to fall in love than was Isabel Lownd. She was tall, active, fair, the very picture of feminine health, with bright grey eyes, a perfectly beautiful nose, — as is common to almost all girls belonging to Craven, — a mouth by no means delicately small, but eager, eloquent, and full of spirit, a well-formed short chin, with a dimple, and light brown hair, which was worn plainly smoothed over her brows, and fell in short curls behind her head. Of Maurice Archer it cannot be said that he was handsome. He had a snub nose; and a man so visaged can hardly be good-looking, though a girl with a snub nose may be very pretty. But he was a well-made young fellow, having a look of power about him, with dark brown hair, cut very short, close shorn, with clear but rather small blue eyes, and an expression of countenance which allowed no one for a moment to think that he was weak in character, or a fool. His own place, called Hundlewick Hall, was about five miles from the parsonage. He had been there four or five times a week since his arrival at Kirkby Cliffe, and had already made arrangements for his own entrance upon the land in the following September. If a marriage were to come of it, the arrangement would be one very comfortable for the father and mother at Kirkby Cliffe. Mrs. Lownd had already admitted as much as that to herself, though she still trembled for her girl. Girls are so prone to lose their hearts, whereas the young men of these days are so very cautious and hard! That, at least, was Mrs. Lownd's idea of girls and young men; and even at this present moment she was hardly happy about her child. Maurice, she was sure, had spoken never a word that might not have been proclaimed from the church tower; but her girl, she thought, was not quite the same as she had been before the young man had come among them. She was somewhat less easy in her manner, more preoccupied, and seemed to labour under a conviction that the presence in the house of Maurice Archer must alter the nature of her life. Of course it had altered the nature of her life, and of course she thought a great deal of Maurice Archer.

It had been chiefly at Mabel's instigation that Isabel had

invited the co-operation of her father's visitor in the adornment of the church for Christmas Day. Isabel had expressed her opinion that Mr. Archer didn't care a bit about such things, but Mabel declared that she had already extracted a promise from him. "He'll do anything I ask him," said Mabel, proudly. Isabel, however, had not cared to undertake the work in such company, simply under her sister's management, and had proffered the request herself. Maurice had not declined the task, — had indeed promised his assistance in some indifferent fashion, — but had accompanied his promise by a suggestion that Christmas was a bore! Isabel had rebuked him, and then he had explained. But his explanation, in Isabel's view of the case, only made the matter worse. Christmas to her was a very great affair indeed, — a festival to which the roast beef and the plum-pudding were, no doubt, very necessary; but not by any means the essence, as he had chosen to consider them. Christmas a bore! No; a man who thought Christmas to be a bore should never be more to her than a mere acquaintance. She listened to his explanation, and then left the room, almost indignantly. Maurice, when she was gone, looked after her, and then read a page of his novel; but he was thinking of Isabel, and not of the book. It was quite true that he had never said a word to her that might not have been declared from the church tower; but, nevertheless, he had thought about her a good the words, assumed that look of which he was already afraid, but said not a word. Then dinner was announced, and he gave his arm to the parson's wife.

Not a word was said about Christmas that evening. Isabel had threatened the young man with her father's displeasure on account of his expressed opinion as to the festival being a bore, but Mr. Lownd was not himself one who talked a great deal about any church festival. Indeed, it may be doubted whether his more enthusiastic daughter did not in her heart think him almost too indifferent on the subject. In the decorations of the church he, being an elderly man, and one with other duties to perform, would of course take no part. When the day came he would preach, no doubt, an appropriate sermon, would then eat his own roast beef and pudding with his ordinary appetite, would afterwards, if allowed to do so, sink into his arm-chair behind his book, — and then, for him, Christmas would be over. In all this there was no disrespect for the day, but it was hardly an enthusiastic observance. Isabel desired to greet the morning of her Saviour's birth with some special demonstration of joy. Perhaps from year to year she was somewhat disappointed, — but never before had it been hinted to her that Christmas was a bore.

On the following morning the work was to be commenced immediately after breakfast. The same thing had been done so often at Kirkby Cliffe, that the rector was quite used to it.

David Drum, the clerk, who was also schoolmaster, and Barty Crossgrain, the parsonage gardener, would devote their services to the work in hand throughout the whole day, under the direction of Isabel. Mabel would of course be there assisting, as would also two daughters of a neighbouring farmer. Mrs. Lownd would go down to the church about eleven, and stay till one, when the whole party would come up to the parsonage for refreshment. Mrs. Lownd would not return to the work, but the others would remain there till it was finished, which finishing was never accomplished till candles had been burned in the church for a couple of hours. Then there would be more refreshments; but on this special day the parsonage dinner was never comfortable and orderly. The rector bore it all with good humour, but no one could say that he was enthusiastic in the matter. Mabel, who delighted in going up ladders, and leaning over the pulpit, and finding herself in all those odd parts of the church to which her imagination would stray during her father's sermons, but which were ordinarily inaccessible to her, took great delight in the work. And perhaps Isabel's delight had commenced with similar feelings. Immediately after breakfast, which was much hurried on the occasion, she put on her hat and hurried down to the church, without a word to Maurice on the subject. There was another whisper from Mabel, which was answered also with a whisper, and then Mabel also went. Maurice took up his novel, and seated himself comfortably by the parlour fire.

But again he did not read a word. Why had Isabel made herself so disagreeable, and why had she perked up her head as she left the room in that self-sufficient way, as though she was determined to show him that she did not want his assistance? Of course, she had understood well enough that he had not intended to say that the ceremonial observance of the day was a bore. He had spoken of the beef and the pudding, and she had chosen to pretend to misunderstand him. He would not go near the church. And as for his love, and his half-formed resolution to make her his wife, he would get over it altogether. If there were one thing more fixed with him than another, it was that on no consideration would he marry a girl who should give herself airs. Among them they might decorate the church as they pleased, and when he should see their handywork, — as he would do, of course, during the services of Christmas Day, — he would pass it by without a remark. So resolving, he again turned over a page or two of his novel, and then remembered that he was bound, at any rate, to keep his promise to his friend Mabel. Assuring himself that it was on that plea that he went, and on no other, he sauntered down to the church.

## KIRKBY CLIFFE CHURCH

Kirkby Cliffe Church stands close upon the River Wharfe, about a quarter of a mile from the parsonage, which is on a steep hill-side running down from the moors to the stream. A prettier little church or graveyard you shall hardly find in England. Here, no large influx of population has necessitated the removal of the last home of the parishioners from beneath the shelter of the parish church. Every inhabitant of Kirkby Cliffe has, when dead, the privilege of rest among those green hillocks. Within the building is still room for tablets commemorative of the rectors and their wives and families, for there are none others in the parish to whom such honour is accorded. Without the walls, here and there, stand the tombstones of the farmers; while the undistinguished graves of the peasants lie about in clusters which, solemn though they be, are still picturesque. The church itself is old, and may probably be doomed before long to that kind of destruction which is called restoration; but hitherto it has been allowed to stand beneath all its weight of ivy, and has known but little change during the last two hundred years. Its old oak pews, and ancient exalted reading-desk and pulpit are offensive to many who come to see the spot; but Isabel Lownd is of the opinion that neither the one nor the other could be touched, in the way of change, without profanation.

In the very porch Maurice Archer met Mabel, with her arms full of ivy branches, attended by David Drum. "So you have come at last, Master Maurice?" she said.

"Come at last! Is that all the thanks I get? Now let me see what it is you're going to do. Is your sister here?"

"Of course she is. Barty is up in the pulpit, sticking holly branches round the sounding-board, and she is with him."

"T' boorde's that rotten an' maaky, it'll be doon on Miss Is'bel's heede, an' Barty Crossgrain ain't more than or'nary saft-handed," said the clerk.

They entered the church, and there it was, just as Mabel had said. The old gardener was standing on the rail of the pulpit, and Isabel was beneath, handing up to him nails and boughs, and giving him directions as to their disposal. "Naa, miss, naa; it wonot do that a-way," said Barty. "Thou'll ha' me o'er on to t'stances — thou wilt, that a-gait. Lard-a-mussy, miss, thou munnot clim' up, or thou'lt be doon, and brek thee banes, thee ull!" So saying, Barty Crossgrain, who had contented himself with remonstrating when called upon by his young mistress to imperil his own neck, jumped on to the floor of the pulpit and took hold of the young lady by both her ankles. As he did so, he looked up at her with anxious eyes, and steadied himself on his own feet, as though it might become necessary for him to perform some great feat of activity. All this Maurice Archer saw, and Isabel saw that he saw it. She was not well pleased at knowing that he should see her in that position, held by the legs by the old gardener, and from which she could only extricate herself by putting her hand on the old man's neck as she jumped down from her perch. But she did jump down, and then began to scold Crossgrain, as though the awkwardness had come from fault of his.

"I've come to help, in spite of the hard words you said to me yesterday, Miss Lownd," said Maurice, standing on the lower steps of the pulpit. "Couldn't I get up and do the things at the top?" But Isabel thought that Mr. Archer could not get up and "do the things at the top." The wood was so far decayed that they must abandon the idea of ornamenting the sounding-board, and so both Crossgrain and Isabel descended into the body of the church.

Things did not go comfortably with them for the next hour. Isabel had certainly invited his co-operation, and therefore could not tell him to go away; and yet, such was her present feeling towards him, she could not employ him profitably, and with ease to herself. She was somewhat angry with him, and more angry with herself. It was not only that she had spoken hard words to him, as he had accused her of doing, but that, after the speaking of the hard words, she had been distant and cold in her manner to him. And yet he was so much to her! she liked him so well! — and though she had never dreamed of admitting to herself that she was in love with him, yet — yet it would be so pleasant to have the opportunity of asking herself whether she could not love him, should he ever give her a fair and open opportunity of searching her own heart on the matter. There had now sprung up some half-quarrel between them, and it was impossible that it could be set aside by any action on her part. She could not be otherwise than cold and haughty in her demeanour to him. Any attempt at reconciliation must come from him, and the longer that she continued to be cold and haughty, the less chance there was that it would come. And yet she knew that she had been right to rebuke him for what he had said. "Christmas a bore!" She would rather lose his friendship for ever than hear such words from his mouth, without letting him know what she thought of them. Now he was there with her, and his coming could not but be taken as a sign of repentance. Yet she could not soften her manners to him, and become intimate with him, and playful, as had been her wont. He was allowed to pull about the masses of ivy, and to stick up branches of holly here and there at discretion; but what he did was done under Mabel's direction, and not under hers, — with the aid of one of the farmer's daughters, and not with her aid. In silence she continued to work round the chancel and communion-table, with Crossgrain, while Archer, Mabel, and David Drum used their taste and told me it was all — a bore. Indeed you said much worse than that. I certainly did not mean to ask you again. Mabel asked you, and you came to oblige her. She talked to you, for I heard her; and I was half disposed to tell her not to laugh so much, and to remember that she was in church."

"I did not laugh, Miss Lownd."

"I was not listening especially to you."

"Confess, now," he said after a pause; "don't you know that you misinterpreted me yesterday, and that you took what I said in a different spirit from my own."

"No; I do not know it."

"But you did. I was speaking of the holiday part of Christmas, which consists of pudding and beef, and is surely subject to ridicule, if one chooses to ridicule pudding and beef. You answered me as though I had spoken slightingly of the religious feeling which belongs to the day."

"You said that the whole thing was — ; I won't repeat the word. Why should pudding and beef be a bore to you, when it is prepared as a sign that there shall be plenty on that day for people who perhaps don't have plenty on any other day of the year? The meaning of it is, that you don't like it all, because that which gives unusual enjoyment to poor people, who very seldom have any pleasure, is tedious to you. I don't like you for feeling it to be tedious. There! that's the truth. I don't mean to be uncivil, but —— "

"You are very uncivil."

"What am I to say, when you come and ask me?"

"I do not well know how you could be more uncivil, Miss Lownd. Of course it is the commonest thing in the world, that one person should dislike another. It occurs every day, and people know it of each other. I can perceive very well that you dislike me, and I have no reason to be angry with you for disliking me. You have a right to dislike me, if your mind runs that way. But it is very unusual for one person to tell another so to his face, — and more unusual to say so to a guest." Maurice Archer, as he said this, spoke with a degree of solemnity to which she was not at all accustomed, so that she became frightened at what she had said. And not only was she frightened, but very unhappy also. She did not quite know whether she had or had not told him plainly that she disliked him, but she was quite sure that she had not intended to do so. She had been determined to scold him, — to let him see that, however much of real friendship there might be between them, she would speak her mind plainly, if he offended her; but she certainly had not desired to give him cause for lasting wrath against her. "However," continued Maurice, "perhaps the truth is best after all, though it is so very unusual to hear such truths spoken."

"I didn't mean to be uncivil," stammered Isabel.

"But you meant to be true?"

"I meant to say what I felt about Christmas Day." Then she paused a moment. "If I have offended you, I beg your pardon."

He looked at her and saw that her eyes were full of tears, and his heart was at once softened towards her. Should he say a word to her, to let her know that there was, — or, at any rate, that henceforth there should be no offence? But it occurred to him that if he did so, that word would mean so much, and would lead perhaps to the saying of other words, which ought not to be shown without forethought. And now, too, they were within the parsonage gate, and there was no time for speaking. "You will go down again after lunch?" he asked.

"I don't know; — not if I can help it. Here's Papa." She had begged his pardon, — had humbled herself before him. And he had not said a word in acknowledgment of the grace she had done him. She almost thought that she did dislike him, — really dislike him. Of course he had known what she meant, and he had chosen to misunderstand her and to take her, as it were, at an advantage. In her difficulty she had abjectly apologised to him, and he had not even deigned to express himself as satisfied with what she had done. She had known him to be conceited and masterful; but that, she had thought, she could forgive, believing it to be the common way with men, — imagining, perhaps, that a man was only the more worthy of love on account of such fault; but now she found that he was ungenerous also, and deficient in that chivalry without which a man can hardly appear at advantage in a woman's eyes. She went on into the house, merely touching her father's arm, as she passed him, and hurried up to her own room. "Is there anything wrong with Isabel?" asked Mr. Lownd.

"She has worked too hard, I think, and is tired," said Maurice.

Within ten minutes they were all assembled in the dining-room, and Mabel was loud in her narrative of the doings of the morning. Barty Crossgrain and David Drum had both declared the sounding-board to be so old that it mustn't even be touched, and she was greatly afraid that it would tumble down some day and "squash papa" in the pulpit. The rector ridiculed the idea of any such disaster; and then there came a full description of the morning's scene, and of Barty's fears lest Isabel should "brek her banes." "His own wig was almost off," said Mabel, "and he gave Isabel such a lug by the leg that she very nearly had to jump into his arms."

"I didn't do anything of the kind," said Isabel.

"You had better leave the sounding-board alone," said the parson.

"We have left it alone, papa," said Isabel, with great dignity. "There are some other things that can't be done this year." For

Isabel was becoming tired of her task, and would not have returned to the church at all could she have avoided it.

"What other things?" demanded Mabel, who was as enthusiastic as ever. "We can finish all the rest. Why shouldn't we finish it? We are ever so much more forward than we were last year, when David and Barty went to dinner. We've finished the Granby-Moore pew, and we never used to get to that till after luncheon." But Mabel on this occasion had all the enthusiasm to herself. The two farmer's daughters, who had been brought up to the parsonage as usual, never on such occasions uttered a word. Mrs. Lownd had completed her part of the work; Maurice could not trust himself to speak on the subject; and Isabel was dumb. Luncheon, however, was soon over, and something must be done. The four girls of course returned to their labours, but Maurice did not go with them, nor did he make any excuse for not doing so.

"I shall walk over to Hundlewick before dinner," he said, as soon as they were all moving. The rector suggested that he would hardly be back in time. "Oh, yes; ten miles — two hours and a half; and I shall have two hours there besides. I must see what they are doing with our own church, and how they mean to keep Christmas there. I'm not quite sure that I shan't go over there again to-morrow." Even Mabel felt that there was something wrong, and said not a word in opposition to this wicked desertion.

He did walk to Hundlewick and back again, and when at Hundlewick he visited the church, though the church was a mile beyond his own farm. And he added something to the store provided for the beef and pudding of those who lived upon his own land; but of this he said nothing on his return to Kirkby Cliffe. He walked his dozen miles, and saw what was being done about the place, and visited the cottages of some who knew him, and yet was back at the parsonage in time for dinner. And during his walk he turned many things over in his thoughts, and endeavoured to make up his mind on one or two points. Isabel had never looked so pretty as when she jumped down into the pulpit, unless it was when she was begging his pardon for her want of courtesy to him. And though she had been, as he described it to himself, "rather down upon him," in regard to what he had said of Christmas, did he not like her the better for having an opinion of her own? And then, as he had stood for a few minutes leaning on his own gate, and looking at his own house at Hundlewick, it had occurred to him that he could hardly live there without a companion. After that he had walked back again, and was dressed for dinner, and in the drawing-room before any one of the family.

With poor Isabel the afternoon had gone much less satisfactorily. She found that she almost hated her work, that she really had a headache, and that she could put no heart into what she was doing. She was cross to Mabel, and almost surly to David Drum and Barty Crossgrain. The two farmer's daughters were allowed to do almost what they pleased with the holly branches, — a state of things which was most unusual, — and then Isabel, on her return to the parsonage, declared her intention of going to bed! Mrs. Lownd, who had never before known her to do such a thing, was perfectly shocked. Go to bed, and not come down the whole of Christmas Eve! But Isabel was resolute. With a bad headache she would be better in bed than up. Were she to attempt to shake it off, she would be ill the next day. She did not want anything to eat, and would not take anything. No; she would not have any tea, but would go to bed at once. And to bed she went.

She was thoroughly discontented with herself, and felt that Maurice had, as it were, made up his mind against her forever. She hardly knew whether to be angry with herself or with him; but she did know very well that she had not intended really to quarrel with him. Of course she had been in earnest in what she had said; but he had taken her words as signifying so much more than she had intended! If he chose to quarrel with her, of course he must; but a friend could not, she was sure, care for her a great deal who would really be angry with her for such a trifle. Of course this friend did not care for her at all, — not the least, or he would not treat her

ANTHONY TROLLOPE

so savagely. He had been quite savage to her, and she hated him for it. And yet she hated herself almost more. What right could she have had first to scold him, and then to tell him to his face that she disliked him? Of course he had gone away to Hundlewick. She would not have been a bit surprised if he had stayed there and never come back again. But he did come back, and she hated herself as she heard their voices as they all went in to dinner without her. It seemed to her that his voice was more cheery than ever. Last night and all the morning he had been silent and almost sullen, but now, the moment that she was away, he could talk and be full of spirits. She heard Mabel's ringing laughter downstairs, and she almost hated Mabel. It seemed to her that everybody was gay and happy because she was upstairs in her bed, and ill. Then there came a peal of laughter. She was glad that she was upstairs in bed, and ill. Nobody would have laughed, nobody would have been gay, had she been there. Maurice Archer liked them all, except her, — she was sure of that. And what could be more natural after her conduct to him? She had taken upon herself to lecture him, and of course he had not chosen to endure it. But of one thing she was quite sure, as she lay there, wretched in her solitude, — that now she would never alter her demeanour to him. He had chosen to be cold to her, and she would be like frozen ice to him. Again and again she heard their voices, and then, sobbing on her pillow, she fell asleep.

## SHOWING HOW
## ISABEL LOWND TOLD A LIE

On the following morning, — Christmas morning, — when she woke, her headache was gone, and she was able, as she dressed, to make some stern resolutions. The ecstasy of her sorrow was over, and she could see how foolish she had been to grieve as she had grieved. After all, what had she lost, or what harm had she done? She had never fancied that the young man was her lover, and she had never wished, — so she now told herself, — that he should become her lover. If one thing was plainer to her than another, it was this — that they two were not fitted for each other. She had sometimes whispered to herself, that if she were to marry at all, she would fain marry a clergyman. Now, no man could be more unlike a clergyman than Maurice Archer. He was, she thought, irreverent, and at no pains to keep his want of reverence out of sight, even in that house. He had said that Christmas was a bore, which, to her thinking, was abominable. Was she so poor a creature as to go to bed and cry for a man who had given her no sign that he even liked her, and of whose ways she disapproved so greatly, that even were he to offer her his hand she would certainly refuse it? She consoled herself for the folly of the preceding evening by assuring herself that she had really worked in the church till she was ill, and that she would have gone to bed, and must have gone to bed, had Maurice Archer never been seen or heard of at the parsonage. Other people went to bed when they had headaches, and why should not she? Then she resolved, as she dressed, that there should be no signs of illness, nor bit of ill-humour on her, on this sacred day. She would appear among them all full of mirth and happiness, and would laugh at the attack brought upon her by Barty Crossgrain's sudden fear in the pulpit; and she would greet Maurice Archer with all possible cordiality, wishing him a merry Christmas as she gave him her hand, and would make him understand in a moment that she had altogether forgotten their mutual bickerings. He should understand that, or should, at least, understand that she willed that it should all be regarded as forgotten. What was he to her, that any thought of him should be allowed to perplex her mind on such a day as this?

She went downstairs, knowing that she was the first up in the house, — the first, excepting the servants. She went into Mabel's room, and kissing her sister, who was only half awake, wished her many, many, many happy Christmases.

"Oh, Bell," said Mabel, "I do so hope you are better!"

"Of course I am better. Of course I am well. There is nothing for a headache like having twelve hours round of sleep. I don't know what made me so tired and so bad."

"I thought it was something Maurice said," suggested Mabel.

"Oh, dear, no. I think Barty had more to do with it than Mr. Archer. The old fellow frightened me so when he made me think I was falling down. But get up, dear. Papa is in his room, and he'll be ready for prayers before you."

Then she descended to the kitchen, and offered her good wishes to all the servants. To Barty, who always breakfasted there on Christmas mornings, she was especially kind, and said something civil about his work in the church.

"She'll 'bout brek her little heart for t' young mon there, an'he's naa true t' her," said Barty, as soon as Miss Lownd had closed the kitchen door; showing, perhaps, that he knew more of the matter concerning herself than she did.

She then went into the parlour to prepare the breakfast, and to put a little present, which she had made for her father, on his plate; — when, whom should she see but Maurice Archer!

It was a fact known to all the household, and a fact that had not recommended him at all to Isabel, that Maurice never did come downstairs in time for morning prayers. He was always the last; and, though in most respects a very active man, seemed to be almost a sluggard in regard to lying in bed late. As far as she could remember at the moment, he had never been present at prayers a single morning since the first after his arrival at the parsonage, when shame, and a natural feeling of strangeness in the house, had brought him out of his bed. Now he was there half an hour before the appointed time, and during that half-hour she was doomed to be alone with him. But her courage did not for a moment desert her.

"This is a wonder!" she said, as she took his hand. "You will have a long Christmas Day, but I sincerely hope that it may be a happy one."

"That depends on you," said he.

"I'll do everything I can," she answered. "You shall only have a very little bit of roast beef, and the unfortunate pudding shan't be brought near you." Then she looked in his face, and saw that his manner was very serious, — almost solemn, — and quite unlike his usual ways. "Is anything wrong?" she asked.

"I don't know; I hope not. There are things which one has to say which seem to be so very difficult when the time comes. Miss Lownd, I want you to love me."

"What!" She started back as she made the exclamation, as though some terrible proposition had wounded her ears. If she had ever dreamed of his asking for her love, she had dreamed of it as a thing that future days might possibly produce; — when he should be altogether settled at Hundlewick, and when they should have got to know each other intimately by the association of years.

"Yes, I want you to love me, and to be my wife. I don't know how to tell you; but I love you better than anything and everything in the world, — better than all the world put together. I have done so from the first moment that I saw you; I have. I knew how it would be the very first instant I saw your dear face, and every word you have spoken, and every look out of your eyes, has made me love you more and more. If I offended you yesterday, I will beg your pardon."

"Oh, no," she said.

"I wish I had bitten my tongue out before I had said what I did about Christmas Day. I do, indeed. I only meant, in a half-joking way, to — to — to ———. But I ought to have known you wouldn't like it, and I beg your pardon. Tell me, Isabel, do you think that you can love me?"

Not half an hour since she had made up her mind that, even were he to propose to her, — which she then knew to be absolutely impossible, — she would certainly refuse him. He was not the sort of man for whom she would be a fitting wife; and she had made up her mind also, at the same time, that she did not at all care for him, and that he certainly did not in the least care for her. And now the offer had absolutely been made to her! Then came across her mind an idea that he ought in the first place to have gone to her father; but as to that she was not quite sure. Be that as it might, there he was, and she must give him some answer. As for thinking about it, that was altogether beyond her. The shock to her was too great to allow of her thinking. After some fashion, which afterwards was quite unintelligible to herself, it seemed to her, at that moment, that duty, and maidenly reserve, and filial obedience, all required her to reject him instantly. Indeed, to have accepted him would have been quite beyond her power. "Dear Isabel," said he, "may I hope that some day you will love me?"

"Oh, Mr. Archer, don't," she said. "Do not ask me."

"Why should I not ask you?"

"It can never be." This she said quite plainly, and in a voice that seemed to him to settle his fate forever; and yet at the moment her heart was full of love towards him. Though she could not think, she could feel. Of course she loved him. At the very moment in which she was telling him that it could never be, she was elated by an almost ecstatic triumph, as she remembered all her fears, and now knew that the man was at her feet.

When a girl first receives the homage of a man's love, and receives it from one whom, whether she loves him or not, she thoroughly respects, her earliest feeling is one of victory, — such a feeling as warmed the heart of a conqueror in the Olympian games. He is the spoil of her spear, the fruit of her prowess, the quarry brought down by her own bow and arrow. She, too, by some power of her own which she is hitherto quite unable to analyse, has stricken a man to the very heart, so as to compel him for the moment to follow wherever she may lead him. So it was with Isabel Lownd as she stood there, conscious of the eager gaze which was fixed upon her face, and fully alive to the anxious tones of her lover's voice. And yet she could only deny him. Afterwards, when she thought of it, she could not imagine why it had been so with her; but, in spite of her great love, she continued to tell herself that there was some obstacle which could never be overcome, — or was it that a certain maidenly reserve sat so strong within her bosom that she could not bring herself to own to him that he was dear to her?

"Never!" exclaimed Maurice, despondently.

"Oh, no!"

"But why not? I will be very frank with you, dear. I did think you liked me a little before that affair in the study." Like him a little! Oh, how she had loved him! She knew it now, and yet not for worlds could she tell him so. "You are not still angry with me, Isabel?"

"No; not angry."

"Why should you say never? Dear Isabel, cannot you try to love me?" Then he attempted to take her hand, but she recoiled at once from his touch, and did feel something of anger against him in that he should thus refuse to take her word. She knew not what it was that she desired of him, but certainly he should not attempt to take her hand, when she told him plainly that she could not love him. A red spot rose to each of her cheeks as again he pressed her. "Do you really mean that you can never, never love me?" She muttered some answer, she knew not what, and then he turned from her, and stood looking out upon the snow which had fallen during the night. She kept her ground for a few seconds, and then escaped through the door, and up to her own bedroom. When once there, she burst out into tears. Could it be possible that she had thrown away forever her own happiness, because she had been too silly to give a true answer to an honest question? And was this the enjoyment and content which she had promised herself for Christmas Day? But surely, surely he would come to her again. If he really loved her as he had declared, if it was true that ever since his arrival at Kirkby Cliffe he had thought of her as his wife, he would not abandon her because in the first tumult of her surprise she had lacked courage to own to him the truth; and then in the midst of her tears there came upon her that delicious recognition of a triumph which, whatever be the victory won, causes such elation to the heart! Nothing, at any rate, could rob her of this — that he had loved her. Then, as a thought suddenly struck her, she ran quickly across the passage, and in a moment was upstairs, telling her tale with her mother's arm close folded round her waist.

In the meantime Mr. Lownd had gone down to the parlour, and had found Maurice still looking out upon the snow. He, too, with some gentle sarcasm, had congratulated the young man on his early rising, as he expressed the ordinary wish of the day. "Yes," said Maurice, "I had something special to do. Many happy Christmases, sir! I don't know much about its being happy to me."

"Why, what ails you?"

"It's a nasty sort of day, isn't it?" said Maurice.

"Does that trouble you? I rather like a little snow on Christmas Day. It has a pleasant, old-fashioned look. And there isn't enough to keep even an old woman at home."

"I dare say not," said Maurice, who was still beating about the bush, having something to tell, but not knowing how to tell it. "Mr. Lownd, I should have come to you first, if it hadn't been for an accident."

"Come to me first! What accident?"

"Yes; only I found Miss Lownd down here this morning, and I asked her to be my wife. You needn't be unhappy about it, sir. She refused me point blank."

"You must have startled her, Maurice. You have startled me, at any rate."

"There was nothing of that sort, Mr. Lownd. She took it all very easily. I think she does take things easily." Poor Isabel! "She just told me plainly that it never could be so, and then she walked out of the room."

"I don't think she expected it, Maurice."

"Oh, dear no! I'm quite sure she didn't. She hadn't thought about me any more than if I were an old dog. I suppose men do make fools of themselves sometimes. I shall get over it, sir."

"Oh, I hope so."

"I shall give up the idea of living here. I couldn't do that. I shall probably sell the property, and go to Africa."

"Go to Africa!"

"Well, yes. It's as good a place as any other, I suppose. It's wild, and a long way off, and all that kind of thing. As this is Christmas, I had better stay here to-day, I suppose."

"Of course you will."

"If you don't mind, I'll be off early to-morrow, sir. It's a kind of thing, you know, that does flurry a man. And then my being here may be disagreeable to her; — not that I suppose she thinks about me any more than if I were an old cow."

It need hardly be remarked that the rector was a much

older man than Maurice Archer, and that he therefore knew the world much better. Nor was he in love. And he had, moreover, the advantage of a much closer knowledge of the young lady's character than could be possessed by the lover. And, as it happened, during the last week, he had been fretted by fears expressed by his wife, — fears which were altogether opposed to Archer's present despondency and African resolutions. Mrs. Lownd had been uneasy, — almost more than uneasy, — lest poor dear Isabel should be stricken at her heart; whereas, in regard to that young man, she didn't believe that he cared a bit for her girl. He ought not to have been brought into the house. But he was there, and what could they do? The rector was of the opinion that things would come straight, — that they would be straightened not by any lover's propensities on the part of his guest, as to which he protested himself to be altogether indifferent, but by his girl's good sense. His Isabel would never allow herself to be seriously affected by a regard for a young man who had made no overtures to her. That was the rector's argument; and perhaps, within his own mind, it was backed by a feeling that, were she so weak, she must stand the consequence. To him it seemed to be an absurd degree of caution that two young people should not be brought together in the same house lest one should fall in love with the other. And he had seen no symptoms of such love. Nevertheless his wife had

maid-servants were standing behind in a line, ready to come in for prayers. Maurice could not but feel that Mrs. Lownd's manner to him was especially affectionate; for, in truth, hitherto she had kept somewhat aloof from him, as though he had been a ravening wolf. Now she held him by the hand, and had a spark of motherly affection in her eyes, as she, too, repeated her Christmas greeting. It might well be so, thought Maurice. Of course she would be more kind to him than ordinary, if she knew that he was a poor blighted individual. It was a thing of course that Isabel should have told her mother, equally a thing of course that he should be pitied and treated tenderly. But on the next day he would be off. Such tenderness as that would kill him.

As they sat at breakfast, they all tried to be very gracious to each other. Mabel was sharp enough to know that something special had happened, but could not quite be sure what it was. Isabel struggled very hard to make little speeches about the day, but cannot be said to have succeeded well. Her mother, who had known at once how it was with her child, and had required no positive answers to direct questions to enable her to assume that Isabel was now devoted to her lover, had told her girl that if the man's love were worth having, he would surely ask her again. "I don't think he will, mamma," Isabel had whispered, with her face half-hidden on her mother's arm. "He must be very unlike other men if he does not," Mrs. Lownd had said, resolving that the opportunity should not be wanting. Now she was very gracious to Maurice, speaking before him as though he were quite one of the family. Her trembling maternal heart had feared him, while she thought that he might be a ravening wolf, who would steal away her daughter's heart, leaving nothing in return; but now that he had proved himself willing to enter the fold as a useful domestic sheep, nothing could be too good for him. The parson himself, seeing all this, understanding every turn in his wife's mind, and painfully anxious that no word might be spoken which should seem to entrap his guest, strove diligently to talk as though nothing was amiss. He spoke of his sermon, and of David Drum, and of the allowance of pudding that was to be given to the inmates of the neighbouring poor-house. There had been a subscription, so as to relieve the rates from the burden of the plum-pudding, and Mr. Lownd thought that the farmers had not been sufficiently liberal. "There's Furness, at Loversloup, gave us half-a-crown. I told him he ought to be ashamed of himself. He declared to me to my face that if he could find puddings for his own bairns, that was enough for him."

"The richest farmer in these parts, Maurice," said Mrs. Lownd.

"He holds above three hundred acres of land, and could stock double as many, if he had them," said the would-be indignant rector, who was thinking a great deal more of his daughter than of the poor-house festival. Maurice answered him with a word or two, but found it very hard to assume any interest in the question of the pudding. Isabel was more hard-hearted, he thought, than even Farmer Furness, of Loversloup. And why should he trouble himself about these people, — he, who intended to sell his acres, and go away to Africa? But he smiled and made some reply, and buttered his toast, and struggled hard to seem as though nothing ailed him.

The parson went down to church before his wife, and Mabel went with him. "Is anything wrong with Maurice Archer?" she asked her father.

"Nothing, I hope," said he.

"Because he doesn't seem to be able to talk this morning."

"Everybody isn't a chatter-box like you, Mab."

"I don't think I chatter more than mamma, or Bell. Do you know, papa, I think Bell has quarrelled with Maurice Archer."

"I hope not. I should be very sorry that there should be any quarrelling at all — particularly on this day. Well, I think you've done it very nicely; and it is none the worse because you've left the sounding-board alone." Then Mabel went over to David Drum's cottage, and asked after the condition of Mrs. Drum's plum-pudding.

ANTHONY TROLLOPE

No one had ventured to ask Maurice Archer whether he would stay in church for the sacrament, but he did. Let us hope that no undue motive of pleasing Isabel Lownd had any effect upon him at such a time. But it did please her. Let us hope also that, as she knelt beside her lover at the low railing, her young heart was not too full of her love. That she had been thinking of him throughout her father's sermon, — thinking of him, then resolving that she would think of him no more, and then thinking of him more than ever, — must be admitted. When her mother had told her that he would come again to her, she had not attempted to assert that, were he to do so, she would again reject him. Her mother knew all her secret, and, should he not come again, her mother would know that she was heart-broken. She had told him positively that she would never love him. She had so told him, knowing well that at the very moment he was dearer to her than all the world beside. Why had she been so wicked as to lie to him? And if now she were punished for her lie by his silence, would she not be served properly? Her mind ran much more on the subject of this great sin which she had committed on that very morning, — that sin against one who loved her so well, and who desired to do good to her, — than on those general arguments in favour of Christian kindness and forbearance which the preacher drew from the texts applicable to Christmas Day. All her father's eloquence was nothing to her. On ordinary occasions he had no more devoted listener; but, on this morning, she could only exercise her spirit by repenting her own unchristian conduct. And then he came and knelt beside her at that sacred moment! It was impossible that he should forgive her, because he could not know that she had sinned against him.

There were certain visits to her poorer friends in the immediate village which, according to custom, she would make after church. When Maurice and Mrs. Lownd went up to the parsonage, she and Mabel made their usual round. They all welcomed her, but they felt that she was not quite herself with them, and even Mabel asked her what ailed her.

"Why should anything ail me? — only I don't like walking in the snow."

Then Mabel took courage. "If there is a secret, Bell, pray tell me. I would tell you any secret."

"I don't know what you mean," said Isabel, almost crossly.

"Is there a secret, Bell? I'm sure there is a secret about Maurice."

"Don't, — don't," said Isabel.

"I do like Maurice so much. Don't you like him?"

"Pray do not talk about him, Mabel."

"I believe he is in love with you, Bell; and, if he is, I think you ought to be in love with him. I don't know how you could have anybody nicer. And he is going to live at Hundlewick, which would be such great fun. Would not papa like it?"

"I don't know. Oh, dear! — oh, dear!" Then she burst out into tears, and walking out of the village, told Mabel the whole truth. Mabel heard it with consternation, and expressed her opinion that, in these circumstances, Maurice would never ask again to make her his wife.

"Then I shall die," said Isabel, frankly.

## SHOWING HOW ISABEL LOWND REPENTED HER FAULT

In spite of her piteous condition and near prospect of death, Isabel Lownd completed her round of visits among her old friends. That Christmas should be kept in some way by every inhabitant of Kirkby Cliffe, was a thing of course. The district is not poor, and plenty on that day was rarely wanting. But Parson Lownd was not what we call a rich man; and there was no resident squire in the parish. The farmers, comprehending well their own privileges, and aware that the obligation of gentle living did not lie on them, were inclined to be close-fisted; and thus there was sometimes a difficulty in providing for the old and the infirm. There was a certain ancient widow in the village, of the name of Mucklewort, who was troubled with three orphan grandchildren and a lame daughter; and Isabel had, some days since, expressed a fear up at the parsonage that the good things of this world might be scarce in the old widow's cottage. Something had, of course, been done for the old woman, but not enough, as Isabel had thought. "My dear," her mother had said, "it is no use trying to make very poor people think that they are not poor."

"It is only one day in the year," Isabel had pleaded.

"What you give in excess to one, you take from another," replied Mrs. Lownd, with the stern wisdom which experience teaches. Poor Isabel could say nothing further, but had feared greatly that the rations in Mrs. Mucklewort's abode would be deficient. She now entered the cottage, and found the whole family at that moment preparing themselves for the consumption of a great Christmas banquet. Mrs. Mucklewort, whose temper was not always the best in the world, was radiant. The children were silent, open-eyed, expectant, and solemn. The lame aunt was in the act of transferring a large lump of beef, which seemed to be commingled in a most inartistic way with potatoes and cabbage, out of a pot on to the family dish. At any rate there was plenty; for no five appetites — had the five all been masculine, adult, and yet youthful — could, by any feats of strength, have emptied that dish at a sitting. And Isabel knew well that there had been pudding. She herself had sent the pudding; but that, as she was well aware, had not been allowed to abide its fate till this late hour of the day. "I'm glad you're all so well employed," said Isabel. "I thought you had done dinner long ago. I won't stop a minute now."

The old woman got up from her chair, and nodded her head, and held out her withered old hand to be shaken. The children opened their mouths wider than ever, and hoped there might be no great delay. The lame aunt curtseyed and explained the circumstances. "Beef, Miss Isabel, do take a mortal time t' boil; and it ain't no wise good for t' bairns to have it any ways raw." To this opinion Isabel gave her full assent, and expressed her gratification that the amount of beef should be sufficient to require so much cooking. Then the truth came out. "Muster Archer just sent us over from Rowdy's a meal's meat with a vengence; God bless him!" "God bless him!" crooned out the old woman, and the children muttered some unintelligible sound, as though aware that duty required them to express some Amen to the prayer of their elders. Now Rowdy was the butcher living at Grassington, some six miles away, — for at Kirkby Cliffe there was no butcher. Isabel smiled all round upon them sweetly, with her eyes full of tears, and then left the cottage without a word.

He had done this because she had expressed a wish that these people should be kindly treated, — had done it without a syllable spoken to her or to any one, — had taken trouble, sending all the way to Grassington for Mrs. Mucklewort's beef! No doubt he had given other people beef, and had whispered no word of his kindness to any one at the rectory. And yet she had taken upon herself to rebuke him, because he had not cared for Christmas Day! As she walked along, silent, holding Mabel's hand, it seemed to her that of all men he was the most perfect. She had rebuked him, and had then told him — with incredible falseness — that she did not like him; and after that, when he had proposed to her in the kindest, noblest manner, she had rejected him, — almost as though he had not been good enough for her! She felt now as though she would like to bite the tongue out of her head for such misbehavior.

"Was not that nice of him?" said Mabel. But Isabel could not answer the question. "I always thought he was like that," continued the younger sister. "If he were my lover, I'd do anything he asked me, because he is so good-natured."

"Don't talk to me," said Isabel. And Mabel, who comprehended something of the condition of her sister's mind, did not say another word on their way back to the parsonage.

It was the rule of the house that on Christmas Day they should dine at four o'clock; — a rule which almost justified the very strong expression with which Maurice first offended the young lady whom he loved. To dine at one or two o'clock is a practice which has its recommendations. It suits the appetite, is healthy, and divides the day into two equal halves, so that no man so dining fancies that his dinner should bring to him an end of his usual occupations. And to dine at six, seven, or eight is well adapted to serve several purposes of life. It is convenient, as inducing that gentle lethargy which will sometimes follow the pleasant act of eating at a time when the work of the day is done; and it is both fashionable and comfortable. But to dine at four is almost worse than not to dine at all. The rule, however, existed at Kirkby Cliffe parsonage in regard to this one special day in the year, and was always obeyed.

On this occasion Isabel did not see her lover from the moment in which he left her at the church door till they met at the table. She had been with her mother, but her mother had said not a word to her about Maurice. Isabel knew very well that they two had walked home together from the church, and she had thought that her best chance lay in the possibility that he would have spoken of what had occurred during the walk. Had this been so, surely her mother would have told her; but not a word had been said; and even with her mother Isabel had been too shamefaced to ask a question. In truth, Isabel's name had not been mentioned between them, nor had any allusion been made to what had taken place during the morning. Mrs. Lownd had been too wise and too wary, — too well aware of what was really due to her daughter, — to bring up the subject herself; and he had been silent, subdued, and almost sullen. If he could not get an acknowledgment of affection from the girl herself, he certainly would not endeavour to extract a cold compliance by the mother's aid. Africa, and a disruption of all the plans of his life, would be better to him than that. But Mrs. Lownd knew very well how it was with him; knew how it was with them both; and was aware that in such a condition things should be allowed to arrange themselves. At dinner, both she and the rector were full of mirth and good humour, and Mabel, with great glee, told the story of Mrs. Muckelwort's dinner. "I don't want to destroy your pleasure," she said, bobbing her head at Maurice; "but it did look so nasty! Beef should always be roast beef on Christmas Day."

"I told the butcher it was to be roast beef," said Maurice, sadly.

"I dare say the little Muckleworts would just as soon have it boiled," said Mrs. Lownd. "Beef is beef to them, and a pot for boiling is an easy apparatus."

"If you had beef, Miss Mab, only once or twice a year," said her father, "you would not care whether it were roast or boiled." But Isabel spoke not a word. She was most anxious to join the conversation about Mrs. Mucklewort, and would have liked much to give testimony to the generosity displayed in regard to quantity; but she found that she could not do it. She was absolutely dumb. Maurice Archer did speak, making, every now and then, a terrible effort to be jocose; but Isabel from first to last was silent. Only by silence could she refrain from a renewed deluge of tears.

In the evening two or three girls came in with their younger brothers, the children of farmers of the better class in the neighbourhood, and the usual attempts were made at jollity. Games were set on foot, in which even the rector joined, instead of going to sleep behind his book, and Mabel, still conscious of her sister's wounds, did her very best to promote the sports. There was blindman's-buff, and hide and seek, and snapdragon, and forfeits, and a certain game with music and chairs, — very prejudicial to the chairs, — in which it was everybody's object to sit down as quickly as possible when the music stopped. In the game Isabel insisted on playing, because she could do that alone. But even to do this was too much for her. The sudden pause could hardly be made without a certain hilarity of spirit, and her spirits were unequal to any exertion. Maurice went through his work like a man, was blinded, did his forfeits, and jostled for the chairs with the greatest diligence; but in the midst of it all he, too, was as solemn as a judge, and never once spoke a single word to Isabel. Mrs. Lownd, who usually was not herself much given to the playing of games, did on this occasion make an effort, and absolutely consented to cry the forfeits; but Mabel was wonderfully quiet, so that the farmer's daughters hardly perceived that there was anything amiss.

It came to pass, after a while, that Isabel had retreated to her room, — not for the night, as it was as yet hardly eight o'clock, — and she certainly would not disappear till the visitors had taken their departure, — a ceremony which was sure to take place with the greatest punctuality at ten, after an early supper. But she had escaped for a while, and in the meantime some frolic was going on which demanded the absence of one of the party from the room, in order that mysteries might be arranged of which the absent one should remain in ignorance. Maurice was thus banished, and desired to remain in desolation for the space of five minutes; but, just as he had taken up his position, Isabel descended with slow, solemn steps, and found him standing at her father's study door. She was passing on, and had almost entered the drawing-room, when he called her. "Miss Lownd," he said. Isabel stopped, but did not speak; she was absolutely beyond speaking. The excitement of the day had been so great, that she was all but overcome by it, and doubted, herself, whether she would be able to keep up appearances till the supper should be over, and she should be relieved for the night. "Would you let me say one word to you?" said Maurice. She bowed her head and went with him into the study.

Five minutes had been allowed for the arrangement of the mysteries, and at the end of the five minutes Maurice was authorized, by the rules of the game, to return to the room. But he did not come, and upon Mabel's suggesting that possibly he might not be able to see his watch in the dark, she was sent to fetch him. She burst into the study, and there she found the truant and her sister, very close, standing together on the hearthrug. "I didn't know you were here, Bell," she exclaimed. Whereupon Maurice, as she declared afterwards, jumped round the table after her, and took her in his arms and kissed her. "But you must come," said Mabel, who accepted the embrace with perfect goodwill.

"Of course you must. Do go, pray, and I'll follow, — almost immediately." Mabel perceived at once that her sister had altogether recovered her voice.

"I'll tell 'em you're coming," said Mabel, vanishing.

"You must go now," said Isabel. "They'll all be away soon, and then you can talk about it." As she spoke, he was standing with his arm round her waist, and Isabel Lownd was the happiest girl in all Craven.

Mrs. Lownd knew all about it from the moment in which Maurice Archer's prolonged absence had become cause of complaint among the players. Her mind had been intent upon the matter, and she had become well aware that it was only necessary that the two young people should be alone together for a few moments. Mabel had entertained great hopes, thinking, however, that perhaps three or four years must be passed in melancholy gloomy doubts before the path of true love could be made to run smooth; but the light had shone upon her as soon as she saw them standing together. The parson knew nothing about it till the supper was over. Then, when the front door was open, and the farmer's daughters had been cautioned not to get themselves more wet than they could help in the falling snow, Maurice said a word to his future father-in-law. "She has consented at last, sir. I hope you have nothing to say against it."

"Not a word," said the parson, grasping the young man's hand, and remembering as he did so, the extension of the time over which that phrase "at last" was supposed to spread itself.

Maurice had been promised some further opportunity of "talking about it," and of course claimed a fulfillment of the promise. There was a difficulty about it, as Isabel, having now been assured of her happiness, was anxious to talk about it all to her mother rather than to him; but he was imperative, and there came at last for him a quarter of an hour of delicious triumph in that very spot on which he had been so scolded for saying that Christmas was a bore. "You were so very sudden," said Isabel, excusing herself for her conduct in the morning.

# The Mistletoe Bough

L ET THE BOYS HAVE IT IF THEY LIKE IT," SAID Mrs. Garrow, pleading to her only daughter on behalf of her two sons.

"Pray don't, mamma," said Elizabeth Garrow. "It only means romping. To me all that is detestable; and I am sure it is not the sort of thing that Miss Holmes would like."

"We always had it at Christmas when we were young."

"But, mamma, the world is so changed!"

The point in dispute was one very delicate in its nature, hardly to be discussed in all its bearings even in fiction, and the very mention of which between a mother and daughter showed a great amount of close confidence between them. It was no less than this, — should that branch of mistletoe which Frank Garrow had brought home with him out of the Lowther woods be hung up on Christmas Eve in the dining-room at Thwaite Hall, according to his wishes, or should permission for such hanging be positively refused? It was clearly a thing not to be done after such a discussion, and therefore the decision given by Mrs. Garrow was against it.

I am inclined to think that Miss Garrow was right in saying that the world is changed as touching mistletoe boughs. Kissing, I fear, is less innocent now than it used to be when our grandmothers were alive, and we have become more fastidious in our amusements. Nevertheless, I think that she laid herself fairly open to the raillery with which her brothers attacked her.

"'Honi soit qui mal y pense,'" said Frank, who was eighteen.

"Nobody will want to kiss you, my Lady Fineairs," said Harry, who was just a year younger.

"Because you choose to be a Puritan there are to be no more cakes and ale in the house," said Frank.

"'Still waters run deep,' we all know that," said Harry.

The boys had not been present when the matter was discussed and decided between Mrs. Garrow and her daughter, nor had the mother been present when those little amenities had passed between the brother and sister.

"Only that mamma has said it, and I wouldn't seem to go against her," said Frank, "I'd ask my father. He wouldn't give way to such nonsense, I know."

Elizabeth turned away without answering, and left the

room. Her eyes were full of tears, but she would not let her brothers see that they had vexed her. They were only two days home from school, and for the last week before their coming all her thoughts had been to prepare for their Christmas pleasures. She had arranged their rooms, making everything warm and pretty. Out of her own pocket she had bought a shotbelt for one and skates for the other. She had told the old groom that her pony was to belong exclusively to Master Harry for the holidays, and now Harry told her that "still waters run deep." She had been driven to the use of all her eloquence in inducing her father to purchase that gun for Frank, and now Frank called her a Puritan. And why? She did not choose that a mistletoe bough should be hung in her father's hall when Godfrey Holmes was coming there to visit him. She could not explain this to Frank, but Frank might have had the wit to understand it. But Frank was thinking only of Patty Coverdale, a blue-eyed little romp of sixteen, who, with her sister Kate, was coming from Penrith to spend the Christmas at Thwaite Hall. Elizabeth left the room with her slow, graceful step, hiding her tears — hiding all emotion, as, latterly, she had taught herself that it was feminine to do. "There goes my 'Lady Fineairs'!" said Harry, sending his shrill voice after her.

Thwaite Hall was not a place of much pretension. It was a moderate-sized house, surrounded by pretty gardens and shrubberies, close down upon the River Eamont, on the Westmorland side of the river, looking over to a lovely wooded bank in Cumberland. All the world knows that the Eamont runs out of Ulleswater, dividing the two counties, passing under Penrith Bridge and by the old ruins of Brougham Castle, below which it joins the Eden. Thwaite Hall nestled down close upon the clear rocky stream, about halfway between Ulleswater and Penrith, and had been built just at a bend of the river. The windows of the dining-parlour and of the drawing-room stood at right angles to each other, and yet each commanded a reach of the stream. Immediately from a side door of the house steps were cut down through the red rock to the water's edge, and here a small boat was always moored to a chain. The chain was stretched across the river, fixed on to staples driven into the rock on either side, and thus the boat was pulled backwards and forwards over the stream without aid from oars or paddles. From the opposite side a path led through the wood and across the fields to Penrith, and this was the route commonly used between Thwaite Hall and the town.

Major Garrow was a retired officer of Engineers who had seen service in all parts of the world, and was now spending the evening of his days on a small property which had come to him from his father. He held in his own hands about forty acres of land, and he was the owner of one small farm close by, which was let to a tenant. That, together with his halfpay and the interest of his wife's thousand pounds, sufficed to educate his children, and keep the wolf at a comfortable distance from his door. He himself was a spare thin man, with quiet, lazy, literary habits. He had done the work of life, but had so done it as to permit of his enjoying that which was left to him. His sole remaining care was the establishment of his children, and, as far as he could see, he had no ground for anticipating disappointment. They were clever, good-looking, well-disposed young people, and, upon the whole, it may be said that the sun shone brightly on Thwaite Hall. Of Mrs. Garrow it may certainly be said that she deserved such sunshine.

In years past it had been the practice of the family to have some sort of gathering at Thwaite Hall during Christmas. Godfrey Holmes had been left under the care of Major Garrow, and, as he had always spent his Christmas holidays with his guardian, this, perhaps, had given rise to the practice. Then the Coverdales were cousins of the Garrows, and they had usually been there as children. At the Christmas last past the custom had been broken, for young Holmes had been abroad. Previous to that they had all been children, except him. But, now that they were to meet again, they were no longer children. Elizabeth, at any rate, was not so, for she had already counted nineteen summers. And Isabella

Holmes was coming. Isabella was two years older than Elizabeth, and had been educated in Brussels. Moreover, she was comparatively a stranger at Thwaite Hall, never having been at those early Christmas meetings.

And now I must take permission to begin my story by telling a lady's secret. Elizabeth Garrow had already been in love with Godfrey Holmes; — or perhaps it might be more becoming to say that Godfrey Holmes had already been in love with her. They had already been engaged. And, alas! they had already agreed that that engagement should be broken off. Young Holmes was now twenty-seven years of age, and was employed in a bank at Liverpool, — not as a clerk, but as assistant manager, with a large salary. He was a man well to do in the world, who had money also of his own, and who might afford to marry. Some two years since, on the eve of his leaving Thwaite Hall, he had, with low doubting whisper, told Elizabeth that he loved her, and she had flown trembling to her mother. "Godfrey, my boy," the Major had said to him, as he parted with him the next morning, "Bessy is only a child, and too young to think of this yet." At the next Christmas Godfrey was in Italy, and the thing was gone by; so at least the father and mother said to each other. But the young people had met in the summer, and one joyful letter had come from the girl home to her mother — "I have accepted him, dearest, dearest, mamma! I do love him! But don't tell papa yet, for I have not quite accepted him. I think I am sure, but I am not quite sure. I am not quite sure about him." And then, two days after that, there had come a letter that was not at all joyful — "Dearest mamma, — It is not to be. It is not written in the book. We have both agreed that it will not do. I am so glad that you have not told dear papa, for I could never make him understand. You will understand, for I shall tell you everything, down to his very words. But we have agreed that there shall be no quarrel. It shall be exactly as it was; and he will come at Christmas all the same. It would never do that he and papa should be separated; nor could we now put off Isabella. It is better so in every way, for there is, and need be, no quarrel. We still like each other. I am sure I like him; but I know that I should not make him happy as his wife. He says it is my fault. I, at any rate, have never told him that I thought it his." From all which it will be seen that the confidence between the mother and daughter was very close.

Elizabeth Garrow was a very good girl, but it might almost be a question whether she was not too good. She had learned, or thought that she had learned, that most girls are vapid, silly, and useless — given chiefly to pleasure-seeking and a hankering after lovers, — and she had resolved that she would not be such a one. Industry, self-denial, and a religious purpose in life, were the tasks which she set herself; and she went about the performance of them with much courage. But such tasks, though they are excellently well adapted to fit a young lady for the work of living, may also, if carried too far, have the effect of unfitting her for that work. When Elizabeth Garrow made up her mind that the finding of a husband was not the *summum bonum* of life, she did very well. It is very well that a young lady should feel herself capable of going through the world happily without one. But in teaching herself thus she also taught herself to think that there was a certain merit in refusing herself the natural delight of a lover, even though the possession of the lover were compatible with all her duties to herself, her father and mother, and the world at large. It was not that she had determined to have no lover. She made no such resolve, and when the proper lover came he was admitted to her heart. But she declared to herself, unconsciously, that she must put a guard upon herself lest she should be betrayed into weakness by her own happiness. She had resolved that in loving her lord she would not worship him, and that in giving her heart she would only so give it as it should be given to a human creature like herself. She had acted on these high resolves, and hence it had come to pass, not unnaturally, that Mr. Godfrey Holmes had told her that it was "her fault." She had resolved not to worship her lover, and he, perhaps, had resolved that he would be worshipped.

She was a pretty, fair girl, with soft dark brown hair, and

soft long dark eyelashes. Her grey eyes were tender and lustrous, her face was oval, and the lines of her cheek and chin perfect in their symmetry. She was generally quiet in her demeanour; but when stirred she could rouse herself to great energy, and speak with feeling and almost with fire. Her fault was too great a reverence for martyrdom in general, and a feeling, of which she was unconscious, that it became a young woman to be unhappy in secret — that it became a young woman, I might rather say, to have a source of unhappiness hidden from the world in general and endured without any flaw to her outward cheerfulness. We know the story of the Spartan boy who held the fox under his tunic. The fox was biting him into the very entrails, but the young hero spoke never a word. Now, Bessy Garrow was inclined to think that it was a good thing to have a fox always biting, so that the torment caused no ruffle to her outward smiles. Now, at this moment the fox within her bosom was biting her sore enough, but she bore it without flinching.

"If you would rather that he should not come I will have it arranged," her mother said to her.

"Not for worlds!" she had answered; "I should never think well of myself again."

Her mother had changed her own mind more than once as to the conduct in this matter which it might be best for her to follow, thinking solely of her daughter's welfare. "If he comes they will be reconciled, and she will be happy," had been her first idea. But then there was a stern fixedness of purpose in Bessy's words when she spoke of Mr. Holmes which had expelled this hope, and Mrs. Garrow had for a while thought it better that the young man should not come. But Bessy would not permit this. It would vex her father, put out of course the arrangements of other people, and display weakness on her own part. He should come, and she would endure without flinching while the fox gnawed at her heart.

That battle of the mistletoe had been fought on the morning before Christmas Day, and the Holmeses came on Christmas Eve. Isabella was comparatively a stranger, and therefore received at first the greater share of attention. She and Elizabeth had once seen each other, and for the last year or two had corresponded, but personally they had never been intimate. Unfortunately for Elizabeth that story of Godfrey's offer and acceptance had been communicated to Isabella, as had of course the immediately subsequent story of their separation. But now it would be impossible to avoid the subject in conversation. "Dearest Isabella, let it be as though it never had been," she had said in one of her letters. But sometimes it is very difficult to let things be as though they never had been.

The first evening passed over very well. The two Coverdale girls were there, and there was much talking and merry laughter, rather juvenile in its nature, but, on the whole, none the worse for that. Isabella Holmes was a fine, tall, handsome girl, good-humoured and well disposed to be pleased, rather Frenchified in her manners, and quite able to take care of herself. But she was not above round games, and did not turn up her nose at the boys. Godfrey behaved himself excellently, talking much to the Major, but by no means avoiding Miss Garrow. Mrs. Garrow, though she had known him since he was a boy, had taken an aversion to him since he had quarrelled with her daughter; but there was no room on this first night for showing such aversion, and everything went off well.

"Godfrey is very much improved," the Major said to his wife that night.

"Do you think so?"

"Indeed, I do. He has filled out and become a fine man."

"In personal appearance you mean. Yes, he is well-looking enough."

"And in his manner, too. He is doing uncommonly well at Liverpool, I can tell you; and if he should think of Bessy" —

"There is nothing of that sort," said Mrs. Garrow.

"He did speak to me, you know — two years ago. Bessy was too young then, and so, indeed, was he. But if she likes him" —

"I don't think she does."

ANTHONY TROLLOPE

"Then there's an end of it." And so they went to bed.

"Frank," said the sister to her elder brother, knocking at his door when they had all gone upstairs, "may I come in, if you're not in bed yet?"

"In bed!" said he, looking up with some little pride from his Greek book. "I've one hundred and fifty lines to do before I can get to bed. It'll be two, I suppose. I've got to read uncommon hard these holidays. I've only one more half, you know, and then" —

"Don't overdo it, Frank."

"No. I won't overdo it. I mean to take one day a week as a holiday, and work eight hours a day on the other five. That will be forty hours a week, and will give me just two hundred hours for the holiday. I've got it all down here on a table. That will be a hundred and five for Greek play, forty for algebra" — And so he explained to her the exact destiny of all his long hours of proposed labour. He had as yet been home a day and a half, and had succeeded in drawing out with red lines and blue figures the table which he showed her. "If I can do that it will be pretty well; won't it?"

"But, Frank, you have come for your holidays, to enjoy yourself?"

"But a fellow must work nowadays."

"Don't overdo it, dear; that's all. But, Frank, I could not

130

sleep if I went to bed without speaking to you. You made me unhappy to-day."

"Did I, Bessy?"

"You called me a Puritan, and then you quoted that ill-natured French proverb at me. Do you really believe that your sister thinks evil, Frank?" And as she spoke she put her arm caressingly round his neck.

"Of course I don't."

"Then why say so? Harry is so much younger and so thoughtless that I can bear what he says without so much suffering. But if you and I are not friends I shall be very wretched. If you knew how I have looked forward to your coming home!"

"I did not mean to vex you, and I won't say such things again."

"There's my own Frank! What I said to mamma I said because I thought it right; but you must not say that I am a Puritan. I would do anything in my power to make your holidays bright and pleasant. I know that boys require so much more to amuse them than girls do. Good night, dearest. Pray don't overdo yourself with work, and do take care of your eyes." So saying, she kissed him, and went her way. In twenty minutes after that he had gone to sleep over his book, and, when he woke up to find the candle guttering down, he resolved that he would not begin his measured hours till Christmas Day was fairly over.

The morning of Christmas Day passed very quietly. They all went to church, and then sat round the fire chatting till the four o'clock dinner was ready. The Coverdale girls thought it was rather more dull than former Thwaite Hall festivities, and Frank was seen to yawn. But then everybody knows that the real fun of Christmas never begins till the day itself be passed. The beef and pudding are ponderous, and unless there be absolute children in the party there is a difficulty in grafting any special afternoon amusements on the Sunday pursuits of the morning. In the evening they were to have a dance; — that had been distinctly promised to Patty Coverdale; but the dance would not commence till eight. The beef and pudding were ponderous, but with due efforts they were overcome and disappeared. The glass of port was sipped, the almonds and raisins were nibbled, and then the ladies left the room. Ten minutes after that Elizabeth found herself seated with Isabella Holmes over the fire in her father's little bookroom. It was not by her that this meeting was arranged, for she dreaded such a constrained confidence; but it could not be avoided, and, perhaps, it might be as well now as hereafter.

"Bessy," said the elder girl, "I am dying to be alone with you for a moment."

"Well; you shall not die — that is, if being alone with me will save you."

"I have so much to say to you, and, if you have any true friendship in you, you also will have so much to say to me."

Miss Garrow, perhaps, had no true friendship in her at the moment, for she would gladly have avoided saying anything had that been possible. But in order to prove that she was not deficient in friendship, she gave her friend her hand.

"And now tell me everything about Godfrey," said Isabella.

"Dear Bella, I have nothing to tell, literally nothing."

"That is nonsense. Stop a moment, dear, and understand that I do not mean to offend you. It cannot be that you have nothing to tell if you choose to tell it. You are not the girl to have accepted Godfrey without loving him, nor is he the man to have asked you without loving you. When you wrote me word that you had changed your mind, as you might about a dress, of course I knew you had not told me all. Now I insist upon knowing it — that is, if we are to be friends. I would not speak a word to Godfrey till I had seen you, in order that I might hear your story first."

"Indeed, Bella, there is no story to tell."

"Then I must ask him."

"If you wish to play the part of a true friend to me you will let the matter pass by and say nothing. You must understand that, circumstanced as we are, your brother's visit here —. What I mean is, that it is very difficult for me to act and speak exactly as I should do, and a few unfortunate words spoken may make my position unendurable."

"Will you answer me one question?"

"I cannot tell. I think I will."

"Do you love him?" For a moment or two Bessy remained silent, striving to arrange her words so that they should contain no falsehood, and yet betray no truth. "Ah! I see you do," continued Miss Holmes. "But of course you do. Why else did you accept him?"

"I fancied that I did, as young ladies do sometimes fancy."

"And will you say that you do not, now?" Again Bessy was silent, and then her friend rose from her seat. "I see it all," she said. "What a pity it was that you both had not some friend like me by you at the time! But perhaps it may not be too late."

I need not repeat at length all the protestations which were poured forth with hot energy by poor Bessy. She endeavoured to explain how great had been the difficulty of her position. This Christmas visit had been arranged before that unhappy affair at Liverpool had occurred. Isabella's visit had been partly one of business, it being necessary that certain money affairs should be arranged between her, her brother, and the Major. "I determined," said Bessy, "not to let my own feelings stand in the way, and hoped that things might settle down to their former friendly footing. I already fear that I have been wrong, but it will be ungenerous in you to punish me." Then she went on to say that if anybody attempted to interfere with her she should at once go away to her mother's sister, who lived at Hexham, in Northumberland.

Then came the dance, and the hearts of Kate and Patty Coverdale were at last made happy. But here again poor Bessy was made to understand how terribly difficult was this experiment of entertaining on a footing of friendship a lover with whom she had quarrelled only a month or two before. That she must as a necessity become the partner of Godfrey Holmes she had already calculated, and so much she was prepared to endure. Her brothers would, of course, dance with the Coverdale girls; and her father would, of course, stand up with Isabella. There was no other possible arrangement, — at any rate as a beginning. She had schooled herself, too, as to the way in which she would speak to him on the occasion, and how she would remain mistress of herself and of her thoughts. But when the time came the difficulty was almost too much for her.

"You do not care much for dancing, if I remember?" said he.

"Oh yes, I do. Not as Patty Coverdale does; it's a passion

with her. But then I'm older than Patty Coverdale." After that he was silent for a minute or two.

"It seems so odd for me to be here again," he said. It was odd. She felt that it was odd. But he ought not to have said so.

"Two years make a great difference; the boys have grown so much."

"Yes; and there are other things."

"Bella was never here before, — at least not with you."

"No; but I did not exactly mean that. All that would not make the place so strange. But your mother seems altered to me —. She used to be almost like my own mother."

"I suppose she finds that you are a more formidable person as you grow older. It was all very well scolding you when you were a clerk in the bank, but it does not do to scold the manager. Those are the penalties men pay for becoming great."

"It is not my greatness that stands in my way, but" —

"Then I'm sure I cannot say what it is. But Patty will scold you if you do not mind the figure, though you were the whole board of directors packed into one."

When Bessy went to bed that night she began to feel that she had attempted too much. "Mamma," she said, "could I not make some excuse, and go away to aunt Mary?"

"What, now!"

"Yes, mamma. Now — to-morrow. I need not say that it will make me unhappy to be away at such a time; but I begin to think that it will be better."

"What will papa say?"

"You must tell him all."

"And aunt Mary must be told, also. You would not like that. Has he said anything?"

"No, nothing; — very little, that is. But Bella has spoken to me. Oh! mamma, I think we have been wrong in this: that is, I have been wrong. I feel as though I should disgrace myself, and turn the whole party here into a misfortune."

It would be dreadful, that telling of the story, even though her mother should undertake the task. "I will remain if it be possible," she said; "but, mamma, if I wish to go, you will not stop me?" Her mother promised that she would not stop her, but strongly advised her to stand her ground.

On the following morning, when she came downstairs before breakfast, she found Frank standing in the hall with his gun, of which he was trying the lock. "It is not loaded, is it, Frank?" said she.

"Oh dear no! No one thinks of loading nowadays till one has got out of the house. Directly after breakfast I am going across with Godfrey to the back of Greystock to see after some moor fowl. He asked me to go, and I couldn't well refuse."

"Of course not. Why should you?"

"It will be deuced hard work to make up the time. I was to have been up at four this morning, but that alarum went off and never woke me. However, I shall be able to do something to-night."

"Don't make a slavery of your holidays, Frank. What's the good of having a new gun if you're not to enjoy it?"

"It's not the new gun. I'm not such a child as that comes to. But you see Godfrey is here, and one ought to be civil to him. I'll tell you what I want you girls to do, Bessy. You must come and meet us on our way home. Come over in the boat, and along the path to the Patterdale road. We'll be there under the hill at about five."

"And, if you are not there, are we to wait in the snow?"

"Don't make difficulties, Bessy. I tell you we will be there. We are to go in the cart, and so shall have plenty of time."

"And how do you know the other girls will go?"

"Why, to tell you the truth, Patty Coverdale has promised. As for Miss Holmes, if she won't, why, you must leave her at home with mamma. But Kate and Patty can't come without you."

"Your discretion has found that out, has it?"

"Well, Patty says so. But you will come, won't you, Bessy? As for waiting, it's all nonsense. Of course you can walk on. But we'll be at the stile by five. I've got my watch, you know."

And then Bessy promised him. What would she not have done for him that was in her power to do?

"Go! of course I'll go!" said Miss Holmes; "I'm up to anything. I'd have gone with them in the morning, and have taken a gun, if they had asked me. But, by-the-by, I'd better not."

"Why not?" said Patty, who was hardly yet without fear lest something should mar the expedition.

"What will three gentlemen do with four ladies?"

"Oh, I forgot," said Patty, innocently.

"I'm sure I don't care," said Kate. "You may have Harry if you like."

"Thank you for nothing," said Miss Holmes. "I want one for myself. It's all very well for you to make the offer; but what should I do if Harry wouldn't have me? There are two sides, you know, to every bargain."

"I'm sure he isn't anything to me," said Kate. "Why, he is not quite seventeen yet."

"Poor boy! What a shame to dispose of him so soon! We'll let him off for a year or two; won't we, Miss Coverdale? But as there seems, by acknowledgment, to be one beau with unappropriated services" —

"I'm sure I have appropriated nobody," said Patty, "and don't intend."

"Godfrey, then, is the only knight whose services are claimed," said Miss Holmes, looking at Bessy. Bessy made no immediate answer with either her eyes or tongue, but when the Coverdales were gone she took her new friend to task.

"How can you fill those young girls' heads with such nonsense?"

"Nature has done that, my dear."

"But Nature should be trained, should it not? You will make them think that those foolish boys are in love with them."

"They'll be sure to think that without any teaching from me. The foolish boys, as you call them, will look after that themselves. It seems to me that the foolish boys know what they are about better than some of their elders." And then, after a moment's pause, she added, "As for my brother, I have no patience with him."

"Pray do not discuss your brother," said Bessy. "And, Bella, unless you wish to drive me away, pray do not speak of him and me together as you did just now."

"Are you so bad as that, that the slightest commonplace joke upsets you? Would not his services be due to you as a matter of course? If you are so sore about it you will betray your secret."

"I have no secret — none, at least, from you, or from mamma; and, indeed, none from him. We were both very foolish, thinking that we knew each other and our own hearts, when we knew neither."

"I hate to hear people talk of knowing their hearts. My idea is that, if you like a young man, and he asks you to marry him, you ought to have him — that is, if there's enough to live on. I don't know what more is wanted. But girls are getting to talk and think as though they were to send their hearts through some fiery furnace of trial before they give them up to a husband's keeping. I'm not at all sure that the French fashion is not the best, and that these things shouldn't be managed by the fathers and mothers, or perhaps by the family lawyers. Girls who are so intent upon knowing their own hearts generally end by knowing nobody's hearts but their own, and then they die old maids."

"Better that than give themselves to the keeping of those they don't know or cannot esteem."

"That's a matter of taste. I mean to take the first that comes, so long as he looks like a gentleman and has no less than eight hundred a year. Now, Godfrey does look like a gentleman, and has nearly double that. If I had such a chance I shouldn't think twice of it."

"And if you had not you would not think of it at all."

"That's the way the wind blows, is it?"

"No, no! Oh, Bella, pray, pray leave me alone. Pray do

not interfere. There is no wind blowing any way. All that I want is your silence and your sympathy."

"Very well. I will be silent and sympathetic as the grave. Only don't imagine that I am cold as the grave also. I don't exactly appreciate your ideas; but, if I can do no good, I will at any rate endeavour to do no harm."

After lunch, at about three, they started on their walk, and managed to ferry themselves over the river. "Oh, do let me, Bessy," said Kate Coverdale; "I understand all about it. Look here, Miss Holmes. You pull the chain through your hands" —

"And inevitably tear your gloves to pieces," said Miss Holmes. Kate certainly had done so, and did not seem to be particularly well pleased with the accident.

"There's a nasty nail in the chain," she said. "I wonder why those stupid boys did not tell us."

Of course they reached the trysting-place much too soon, and were very tired of walking up and down to keep their feet warm before the sportsmen came up; but this was their own fault, seeing that they had reached the stile half an hour before the time fixed.

"I never will go anywhere to meet gentlemen again," said Miss Holmes. "It is most preposterous that ladies should be left in the snow for an hour. Well, young men, what sport have you had?"

"I shot the big black cock," said Harry.

"Did you, indeed?" said Kate Coverdale.

"And there are the feathers out of his tail for you. He dropped them in the water, and I had to go in after them up to my middle; but I told you that I would, so I was determined to get them."

"Oh, you silly, silly boy!" said Kate. "But I'll keep them for ever; I will indeed."

This was said a little apart, for Harry had managed to draw the young lady aside before he presented the feathers.

Frank also had his trophies for Patty, and the tale to tell of his own prowess. In that he was a year older than his brother, he was by a year's growth less ready to tender his present to his lady-love openly in the presence of them all; but he found his opportunity; and then he and Patty went on a little in advance. Kate was deep in her consolations to Harry as to his ducking, and thus they four disposed of themselves. Miss Holmes, therefore, and her brother, and Bessy Garrow were left together in the path, and discussed the performances of the day in a manner that exhibited no very ecstatic interest. So they walked for a mile, and by degree the conversation between them dwindled down almost to silence.

"There is nothing I dislike so much as coming out with people younger than myself," said Miss Holmes; "one always feels so old and dull. Listen to those children, there! They make me think myself an old maiden aunt brought out with them to do propriety."

"Patty won't at all approve if she hears you call her a child."

"Nor shall I approve if she treats me like an old woman." And then she stepped on and joined "the children." "I wouldn't spoil even their sport if I could help it," she said to herself. "But with them I shall only be a temporary nuisance. If I remain behind I shall do permanent injury." And thus Bessy and her old lover were left by themselves.

"I hope you will get on well with Bella," said Godfrey, when they had remained silent for a minute or two.

"Oh, yes; she is so good-natured and light-hearted that everybody must like her. But I fear she must find it very dull here."

"She is never dull anywhere; not even at Liverpool, which, for a young lady, I sometimes think is the dullest place on earth. I know it is for a man."

"A man who has work to do can never be dull; can he?"

"Indeed he can; as dull as death. I am so often enough. I have never been very bright there, Bessy, since you left us."

There was nothing in his calling her Bessy, for it had become a habit with him since they were children, and they had formally agreed that everything between them should be as it had been before that foolish whisper of love had been spoken. Indeed, provision had been made by them specially on this point, so that there need be no awkwardness in their mode of addressing each other. Such provision had seemed to be very prudent, but it hardly had the desired effect on the present occasion.

"I don't know what you mean by brightness," she said, after a pause. "Perhaps it is not intended that people's lives should be what you call bright."

"Life ought to be as bright as we can make it."

"It all depends on the meaning of the word. I suppose we are not very bright here at Thwaite Hall; but yet we think ourselves very happy."

"I'm sure you are," said Godfrey. "I very often think of you here."

"We always think of the places where we've been when we were young," said Bessy. Then again they walked on for some way in silence, and Bessy began to increase her pace with the view of catching the children. The present walk to her was anything but bright, and she reflected with dismay that they were still two miles distant from the ferry.

"Bessy," Godfrey said at last; and then he stopped, doubting how he ought to proceed. She, however, did not say a word, but walked on quickly, as though her only hope were in catching the party before her. But they also were walking quickly; for Bella had determined that she would not be caught.

"Bessy, I must speak to you once of what passed between us at Liverpool."

"Must you?" said she.

"Unless you positively forbid it."

"Stop, Godfrey," she said. And they did stop in the path; for now she no longer thought of putting an end to her embarrassment by overtaking her companions. "If any such words are necessary for your comfort it would hardly become me to forbid them. Were I to do so, you might accuse me afterwards of harshness in your own heart. It must be for you to judge whether it is well to reopen a wound that is nearly healed."

"But with me it is not nearly healed. The wound is open always."

"There are some hurts," she said, "which do not admit of an absolute and perfect cure, unless after long years." As she said this she could not but think how much better was his chance of such perfect cure than her own. With her — so she said to herself — such curing was all but impossible; whereas with him it was almost as impossible that the injury should last.

"Bessy," he said — and he again stopped her in the narrow path, standing immediately before on the way — "you remember all the circumstances that made us part?"

"Yes, I think I remember them."

"And you still think that we were right?"

She paused for a moment before she answered him; but it was only for a moment, and then she spoke quite firmly. "Yes, Godfrey, I do. I have thought about it much since then. I have thought, I fear to no good purpose, about aught else. But I have never thought that we had been unwise in that."

"And yet, I think, you loved me?"

"I am bound to confess I did so, as otherwise I must confess myself a liar. I told you at that time that I loved you, and I told you so truly. But it is better — ten times better — that those who love should part, even though they still should love, than that two should be joined together who are incapable of making each other happy. Remember what you told me."

"I do remember."

"You found yourself unhappy in your engagement, and you said that it was my fault."

"Bessy, there is my hand. If you have ceased to love me, there is an end of it; but if you love me still let all that I then said be forgotten."

"Forgotten, Godfrey! How can it be forgotten? You were unhappy, and it was my fault. My fault — as it would be if I tried to solace a sick child with arithmetic, or feed a dog with grass. I had no right to love you, knowing you as I did, and knowing also that my ways would not be your ways. My punishment I understand, and it is not more than I can bear; but I had hoped that your punishment would have been soon over."

"You are too proud, Bessy."

"That is very likely. Frank says that I am a Puritan, and pride was the worst of their sins."

"Too proud and unbending. In marriage should not the man and woman adapt themselves to each other?"

"When they are married, yes; and every girl who thinks of marrying should know that in very much she must adapt herself to her husband. But I do not think that a woman should be the ivy, to take the direction of every branch of the tree to which she clings. If she does so, what can be her own character? But we must go on, or we shall be too late."

"And you will give me no other answer?"

"None other, Godfrey. Have you not just now, at this very moment, told me that I was too proud? Can it be possible that you should wish to tie yourself for life to female pride? And if you tell me that now, at such a moment as this, what would you tell me in the close intimacy of married life, when the trifles of every day would have worn away the courtesies of the guest and lover?"

There was a sharpness of rebuke in this which Godfrey Holmes could not at the moment overcome. Nevertheless, he knew the girl, and understood the workings of her heart and mind. Now, in her present state, she would be unbending, proud, and almost rough. In that she had much to lose in declining the renewed offer which he made her, she would, as it were, continually prompt herself to be harsh and inflexible. Had he been poor, had she not loved him, had not all good things seemed to have attended the promise of such a marriage, she would have been less suspicious of herself in receiving the offer, and more gracious in replying to it. Had he lost all his money before he came back to her she would have taken him at once; or had he been deprived of an eye or become crippled in his legs she would have done so. But, circumstanced as he was, she had no motive to tenderness. There was an organic defect in her character, which, no doubt, was plainly marked by its own bump on her cranium — the bump of philomartyrdom, as it might properly be called. She had shipwrecked her own happiness in rejecting Godfrey Holmes, but it seemed to her to be the proper thing that a well-behaved young lady should shipwreck her own happiness. In the last month or two she had been tossed about by the waters and was nearly drowned. Now there was beautiful land again close to her, and a strong, pleasant hand stretched out to save her; but, though she had suffered terribly among the waves, she still thought it wrong to be saved. It would be so pleasant to take that hand, — so sweet, so joyous, that it what he believed to be the state of his daughter's feelings. "Now you know it all," said he. "I do believe that she loves me; and, if she does, perhaps she may still listen to you." Major Garrow did not then feel sure that he knew it all. But, when he had fully discussed the matter that night with his wife, then he thought that, perhaps, he had arrived at that knowledge.

On the following morning Bessy learned from the maid at an early hour that Godfrey Holmes had left Thwaite Hall and gone back to Liverpool. To the girl she said nothing on the subject; but she felt herself obliged to say a word or two to Bella. "It is his coming that I regret," she said — "that he should have had the trouble and annoyance for nothing. I acknowledge that it was my fault, and I am very sorry."

"It cannot be helped," said Miss Holmes somewhat gravely. "As to his misfortunes, I presume that his journeys between here and Liverpool are not the worst of them."

After breakfast on that day Bessy was summoned into her father's bookroom, and found him there, and her mother also. "Bessy," said he, "sit down, my dear. You know why Godfrey has left us this morning?" Bessy walked round the room so that in sitting she might be close to her mother, and take her mother's hand in her own.

"I suppose I do, papa," she said.

"He was with me late last night, Bessy; and, when he told me what had passed between you, I agreed with him that he had better go."

"It was better that he should go, papa."

"But he has left a message for you."

"A message, papa!"

"Yes, Bessy; and your mother agreed with me that it had better be given to you. It is this, — that, if you will send him word to come again, he will be here by Twelfth Night. He came before on my invitation, but if he returns it must be on yours."

"Oh, papa, I cannot."

"I do not say that you can; but you should think of it calmly before you refuse. You shall give me your answer on New Year's morning."

"Mamma knows that it would be impossible," said Bessy.

"Not impossible, dearest. I do know that it would be a hard thing to do."

"In such a matter you should do what you believe to be right," said her father.

"If I were to ask him here again it would be telling that I would" —

"Exactly, Bessy; it would be telling him that you would be his wife. He would understand it so, and so would your mother and I. It must be understood altogether."

"But, papa, when we were at Liverpool" —

"I have told him everything, dearest," said Mrs. Garrow.

"I think I understand the whole," said the Major; "and in such a matter as this I will give no advice on either side. But you must remember that, in making up your mind, you must think of him as well as of yourself. If you do love him, — if you feel that as his wife you could not love him, — there is not another word to be said. I need not explain to my daughter that under such circumstances she would be wrong to encourage the visits of a suitor. But your mother says you do love him?"

"Oh, mamma!"

"I will not ask you. But, if you do, — if you have so told him, and allowed him to build up an idea of his life's happiness on such telling, — you will, I think, sin greatly against him by allowing false feminine pride to mar his happiness. When once a girl has confessed to a man that she loves him, the confession and the love together put upon her the burden of a duty towards him which she cannot with impunity throw aside." Then he kissed her, and, bidding her give him a reply on the morning of the New Year, left her with her mother.

She had four days for consideration, and they went past with her by no means easily. Could she have been alone with her mother the struggle would not have been so painful, but there was the necessity that she should talk to Isabella

Holmes, and the necessity also that she should not neglect the Coverdales. None could have been kinder than Bella. She did not speak on the subject till the morning of the last day, and then only in a very few words. "Bessy," she said, "as you are great, be merciful!"

"But I am not great, and it would not be mercy," replied Bessy.

"As to that," said Bella, "he has surely a right to his own opinion."

On that evening she was sitting alone in her room when her mother came to her, and her eyes were red with weeping. Pen and paper were before her as though she were resolved to write, but hitherto no word had been written.

"Well, Bessy," said her mother, sitting down close beside her, "is the deed done?"

"What deed, mamma? Who says that I am to do it?"

"The deed is not the writing, but the resolution to write. Five words will be sufficient, if only those five words may be written."

"It is for one's whole life, mamma; for his life as well as my own."

"True, Bessy; that is quite true. But it is equally true whether you bid him come or allow him to remain away. That task of making up one's mind for life must always at last be done in some special moment of that life."

"Mamma, mamma, tell me what I should do."

But this Mrs. Garrow would not do. "I will write the words for you if you like," she said; "but it is you who must resolve that they shall be written. I cannot bid my darling go away and leave me for another home. I can only say that in my heart I do believe that home would be a happy one."

It was morning before the note was written; but when the morning came Bessy had written it and brought it to her mother. "You must take it to papa," she said. Then she went, and hid herself from all eyes till the noon was passed. "Dear Godfrey," — the letter ran, — "Papa says that you will return on Wednesday if I write to ask you. Do come back to us, — if you wish it. Yours always, Bessy."

"It is as good as though she had filled the sheet," said the Major. But in sending it to Godfrey Holmes he did not omit a few accompanying remarks of his own.

An answer came from Godfrey by return of post, and, on the afternoon of the 6th of January, Frank Garrow drove over to the station at Penrith to meet him. On their way back to Thwaite there grew up a very close confidence between the two future brothers-in-law, and Frank explained with great perspicuity a little plan which he had arranged himself. "As soon as it is dark, so that she won't see, Harry will hang it up in the dining-room," he said; "and mind you go in there before you go anywhere else."

"I am very glad you have come back, Godfrey," said the Major meeting him in the hall. "God bless you, dear Godfrey," said Mrs. Garrow. "You will find Bessy in the dining-room," she whispered; but in so whispering she was quite unconscious of Frank's mistletoe bough.

And so also was Bessy. Nor do I think that she was much more conscious when that interview was over. Godfrey had made all manner of promises to Frank; but when the moment arrived he had found the crisis too important for any special reference to the little bough above his head. Not so, however, Patty Coverdale. "It's a shame," she said, bursting out of the room; "and if I'd known what you had done nothing on earth should have induced me to go in. I will not enter the room again till I know that you have taken it out." Nevertheless, her sister Kate was bold enough to solve the mystery before the evening was over.

# The Two Generals

## A Christmas Story
## of the War in Kentucky

C HRISTMAS OF 1860 IS NOW THREE YEARS
past, and the civil war which was then being commenced in America is still raging without any apparent sign of an end. The prophets of that time who
prophesied the worst never foretold anything so black as
this. On that Christmas day Major Anderson, who then
held the command of the forts in Charleston harbour on the
part of the United States Government, removed his men
and stores from Fort Moultrie to Fort Sumter, thinking that
he might hold the one though not both against any attack
from the people of Charleston, whose State, that of South
Carolina, had seceded five days previously. That was in truth
the beginning of the war, though at that time Mr. Lincoln

was not yet President. He became so on the 4th of March, 1861, and on the 15th of April following Fort Sumter was evacuated by Major Anderson, on the part of the United States Government, under fire from the people of Charleston. So little bloody, however, was that affair that no one was killed in the assault; — though one poor fellow perished in the saluting fire with which the retreating officer was complimented as he retired with the so-called honours of war. During the three years that have since passed, the combatants have better learned the use of their weapons of war. No one can now laugh at them for bloodless battles. Never have the sides of any stream been so bathed in blood as have the shores of those Virginian rivers whose names have lately become familiar to us. None of those old death-dooming generals of Europe whom we have learned to hate for the cold-blooded energy of their trade, — Tilly, Gustavus Adolphus, Frederic, or Napoleon; — none of these ever left so many carcases to the kites as have the Johnsons, Jacksons, and Hookers of the American armies, who come and go so fast, that they are almost forgotten before the armies they have led have melted into clay.

Of all the states of the old union, Virginia has probably suffered the most, but Kentucky has least deserved the suffering which has fallen to her lot. In Kentucky the war has raged hither and thither, every town having been subject to inroads from either army. But she would have been loyal to the Union if she could; — nay, on the whole she has been loyal. She would have thrown off the plague chain of slavery if the prurient virtue of New England would have allowed her to do so by her own means. But virtuous New England was too proud of her own virtue to be content that the work of abolition should thus pass from her hands. Kentucky, when the war was beginning, desired nothing but to go on in her own course. She wished for no sudden change. She grew no cotton. She produced corn and meat, and was a land flowing with milk and honey. Her slaves were not as the slaves of the Southern States. They were few in number; tolerated for a time because their manumission was understood to be of all questions the most difficult; — rarely or never sold from the estates to which they belonged. When the war broke out Kentucky said that she would be neutral. Neutral, — and she lying on the front lines of the contest! Such neutrality was impossible to her, — impossible to any of her children!

Near to the little State capital of Frankfort there lived at that Christmas time of 1860 an old man, Major Reckenthorpe by name, whose life had been marked by many circumstances which had made him well known throughout Kentucky. He had sat for nearly thirty years in the Congress of the United States at Washington, representing his own

State sometimes as senator, and sometimes in the lower house. Though called a major he was by profession a lawyer, and as such had lived successfully. Time had been when friends had thought it possible that he might fill the President's chair; but his name had been too much and too long in men's mouths for that. Who had heard of Lincoln, Pierce, or Polk, two years before they were named as candidates for the Presidency? But Major Reckenthorpe had been known and talked of in Washington longer perhaps than any other living politician.

Upon the whole he had been a good man, serving his country as best he knew how, and adhering honestly to his own political convictions. He had been and now was a slave-owner, but had voted in the Congress of his own State for the abolition of slavery in Kentucky. He had been a passionate man, and had lived not without the stain of blood on his hands, for duels had been familiar to him. But he had lived in a time and in a country in which it had been hardly possible for a leading public man not to be familiar with a pistol. He had been known as one whom no man could attack with impunity; but he had also been known as one who would not willingly attack anyone. Now at the time of which I am writing, he was old, — almost on the shelf, — past his duellings and his strong short invectives on the floors of Congress; but he was a man whom no age could tame, and still he was ever talking, thinking, and planning for the political well-being of his State.

In person he was tall, still upright, stiff, and almost ungainly in his gait, with eager grey eyes which the waters of age could not dim, with short, thick, grizzled hair which age had hardly thinned, but which ever looked rough and uncombed, with large hands, which he stretched out with extended fingers when he spoke vehemently; — and of the Major it may be said that he always spoke with vehemence. But now he was slow in his steps, and infirm on his legs. He suffered from rheumatism, sciatica, and other maladies of the old, which no energy of his own could repress. In these days he was a stern, unhappy, all but broken-hearted old man; for he saw that the work of his life had been wasted.

And he had another grief which at this Christmas of 1860 had already become terrible to him, and which afterwards bowed him with sorrow to the ground. He had two sons, both of whom were then at home with him, having come together under the family roof tree that they might discuss with their father the political position of their country, and especially the position of Kentucky. South Carolina had already seceded, and other Slave States were talking of secession. What should Kentucky do? So the Major's sons, young men of eight-and-twenty and five-and-twenty, met together at their father's house; — they met and quarrelled deeply, as their father had well known would be the case.

The eldest of these sons was at that time the owner of the slaves and land which his father had formerly possessed and farmed. He was a Southern gentleman, living on the produce of slave labour, and as such had learned to vindicate, if not love, that social system which has produced as its result the war which is still raging at this Christmas of 1863. To him this matter of secession or non-secession was of vital import. He was prepared to declare that the wealth of the South was derived from its agriculture, and that its agriculture could only be supported by its slaves. He went further than this, and declared also that no further league was possible between a Southern gentleman and a Puritan from New England. His father, he said, was an old man, and might be excused by reason of his age from any active part in the contest that was coming. But for himself there could be but one duty; — that of supporting the new Confederacy, to which he would belong, with all his strength and with whatever wealth was his own.

The second son had been educated at Westpoint, the great military school of the old United States, and was now an officer in the National Army. Not on that account need it be supposed that he would, as a matter of course, join himself to the Northern side in the war, — to the side which, as being in possession of the capital and the old Government establishments, might claim to possess a right to his military services. A large proportion of the officers in the pay of the United States leagued themselves with Secession, — and it is difficult to see why such an act would be more disgraceful in them than in others. But with Frank Reckenthorpe such was not the case. He declared that he would be loyal to the Government which he served; and in saying so, seemed to imply that the want of such loyalty in any other person, soldier or non-soldier, would be disgraceful, as in his opinion it would have been disgraceful in himself.

"I can understand your feeling," said his brother, who was known as Tom Reckenthorpe, "on the assumption that you think more of being a soldier than of being a man; but not otherwise."

"Even if I were no soldier, I would not be a rebel," said Frank.

"How a man can be a rebel for sticking to his own country, I cannot understand," said Tom.

"Your own country!" said Frank. "Is it to be Kentucky or South Carolina? And is it to be a republic or a monarchy; — or shall we hear of Emperor Davis? You already belong to the greatest nation on earth, and you are preparing yourself to belong to the least; — that is, if you should be successful. Luckily for yourself, you have no chance of success."

"At any rate I will do my best to fight for it."

"Nonsense, Tom," said the old man, who was sitting by.

"It is no nonsense, sir. A man can fight without having been at Westpoint. Whether he can do so after having his spirit drilled and drummed out of him there, I don't know."

"Tom!" said the old man.

"Don't mind him, father," said the younger. "His appetite for fighting will soon be over. Even yet I doubt whether we shall ever see a regiment in arms sent from the Southern States against the Union."

"Do you?" said Tom. "If you stick to your colours, as you say you will, your doubts will soon be set at rest. And I'll tell you what, if your regiment is brought into the field, I trust that I may find myself opposite to it. You have chosen to forget that we are brothers, and you shall find that I can forget it also."

"Tom!" said the father, "you should not say such words as that; at any rate, in my presence."

"It is true, sir," said he. "A man who speaks as he speaks does not belong to Kentucky, and can be no brother of mine. If I were to meet him face to face, I would as soon shoot him as another; — sooner, because he is a renegade."

"You are very wicked, — very wicked," said the old man, rising from his chair, — "very wicked." And then, leaning on his stick, he left the room.

"Indeed, what he says is true," said a sweet, soft voice

from a sofa in the far corner of the room. "Tom, you are very wicked to speak to your brother thus. Would you take on yourself the part of Cain?"

"He is more silly than wicked, Ada," said the soldier. "He will have no chance of shooting me, or of seeing me shot. He may succeed in getting himself locked up as a rebel; but I doubt whether he'll ever go beyond that."

"If I ever find myself opposite to you with a pistol in my grasp," said the elder brother, "may my right hand — "

But his voice was stopped, and the imprecation remained unuttered. The girl who had spoken rushed from her seat and put her hand before his mouth. "Tom," she said, "I will never speak to you again if you utter such an oath, — never." And her eyes flashed fire at his and made him dumb.

Ada Forster called Mrs. Reckenthorpe her aunt, but the connection between them was not so near as that of aunt and niece. Ada nevertheless lived with the Reckenthorpes, and had done so for the last two years. She was an orphan, and on the death of her father had followed her father's sister-in-law from Maine down to Kentucky; — for Mrs. Reckenthorpe had come from that farthest and most straitlaced State of the Union, in which people bind themselves by law to drink neither beer, wine, nor spirits, and all go to bed at nine o'clock. But Ada Forster was an heiress, and therefore it was thought well by the elder Reckenthorpes that she should marry one of their sons. Ada Forster was also a beauty, with slim, tall form, very pleasant to the eye; with bright, speaking eyes and glossy hair; with ivory teeth of the whitest, — only to be seen now and then when a smile could be won from her; and therefore such a match was thought desirable also by the younger Reckenthorpes. But unfortunately it had been thought desirable by each of them, whereas the father and mother had intended Ada for the soldier.

I have not space in this short story to tell how progress had been made in the troubles of this love affair. So it was now, that Ada had consented to become the wife of the elder brother, — of Tom Reckenthorpe, with his home among the slaves, — although she, with all her New England feelings strong about her, hated slavery and all its adjuncts. But when has Love stayed to be guided by any such consideration as that? Tom Reckenthorpe was a handsome, high-spirited, intelligent man. So was his brother Frank. But Tom Reckenthorpe could be soft to a woman, and in that, I think, had he found the means of his success. Frank Reckenthorpe was never soft.

Frank had gone angrily from home when, some three months since, Ada had told him her determination. His brother had been then absent, and they had not met till this their Christmas meeting. Now it had been understood between them, by the intervention of their mother, that they would say nothing to each other as to Ada Forster. The elder had, of course, no cause for saying aught, and Frank was too proud to wish to speak on such a matter before his successful rival. But Frank had not given up the battle. When Ada had made her speech to him, he had told her that he would not take it as conclusive. "The whole tenor of Tom's life," he had said to her, "must be distasteful to you. It is impossible that you should live as the wife of a slaveowner."

"In a few years there will be no slaves in Kentucky," she had answered.

"Wait till then," he had answered; "and I also will wait." And so he had left her, resolving that he would bide his time. He thought that the right still remained to him of seeking Ada's hand, although she had told him that she loved his brother. "I know that such a marriage would make each of them miserable," he said to himself over and over again. And now that these terrible times had come upon them, and that he was going one way with the Union, while his brother was going the other way with Secession, he felt more strongly than ever that he might still be successful. The political predilections of American women are as strong as those of American men. And Frank Reckenthorpe knew that all Ada's feelings were as strongly in favour of the Union as his own. Had not she been born and bred in Maine? Was she not ever keen for total abolition, till even the old Major, with all his gallantry for womanhood and all his love for the young girl who had come to his house in his old age, would be driven occasionally by stress of feeling to rebuke her? Frank Reckenthorpe was patient, hopeful, and firm. The time must come when Ada would learn that she could not be a fit wife for his brother. The time had, he thought, perhaps come already; and so he spoke to her a word or two on the evening of that day on which she had laid her hand upon his brother's mouth.

"Ada," he had said, "there are bad times coming to us."

"Good times, I hope," she had answered. "No one could expect that the thing could be done without some struggle. When the struggle has passed we shall say that good times have come." The thing of which she spoke was that little thing of which she was ever thinking, the enfranchisement of four millions of slaves.

"I fear that there will be bad times first. Of course I am thinking of you now."

"Bad or good they will not be worse to me than to others."

"They would be very bad to you if this State were to secede, and if you were to join your lot to my brother's. In the first place, all your fortune would be lost to him and to you."

"I do not see that; but of course I will caution him that it may be so. If it alters his views, I shall hold him free to act as he chooses."

"But Ada, should it not alter yours?"

"What, — because of my money? — or because Tom could not afford to marry a girl without a fortune?"

"I did not mean that. He might decide that for himself. But your marriage with him under such circumstances as those which he now contemplates, would be as though you married a Spaniard or a Greek adventurer. You would be without country, without home, without fortune, and without standing-ground in the world. Look you, Ada, before you answer. I frankly own that I tell you this because I want you to be my wife, and not his."

"Never, Frank; I shall never be your wife, — whether I marry him or no."

"All I ask of you now is to pause. This is no time for marrying or for giving in marriage."

"There I agree with you; but as my word is pledged to him, I shall let him be my adviser in that."

Late on that same night Ada saw her betrothed and bade him adieu. She bade him adieu with many tears, for he came to tell her that he intended to leave Frankfort very early on the following morning. "My staying here now is out of the question," said he. "I am resolved to secede, whatever the State may do. My father is resolved against secession. It is necessary, therefore, that we should part. I have already left my father and mother, and now I have come to say good-bye to you."

"And your brother, Tom?"

"I shall not see my brother again."

"And is that well after such words as you have spoken to each other? Perhaps it may be that you will never see him again. Do you remember what you threatened?"

"I do remember what I threatened."

"And did you mean it?"

"No; of course I did not mean it. You, Ada, have heard me speak many angry words, but I do not think that you have known me do many angry things."

"Never one, Tom: — never. See him then before you go, and tell him so."

"No, — he is hard as iron, and would take any such telling from me amiss. He must go his way, and I mine."

"But though you differ as men, Tom, you need not hate each other as brothers."

"It will be better that we should not meet again. The truth is, Ada, that he always despises anyone who does not think as he thinks. If I offered him my hand he would take it, but while doing so he would let me know that he thought me a fool. Then I should be angry, and threaten him again, and things would be worse. You must not quarrel with me, Ada, if I say that he has all the faults of a Yankee."

"And the virtues too, sir, while you have all the faults of a or two of the very moment at which they were speaking. They must part, and before parting must make some mutual promise as to their future meeting. Marriage now, as things stood at this Christmas time, could not be thought of even by Tom Reckenthorpe. At last he promised that if he were then alive he would be with her again, at the old family house in Frankfort, on the next coming Christmas day. So he went, and as he let himself out of the old house Ada, with her eyes full of tears, took herself up to her bedroom.

During the year that followed — the year 1861 — the American war progressed only as a school for fighting. The most memorable action was that of Bull's Run, in which both sides ran away, not from individual cowardice in either set of men, but from that feeling of panic which is engendered by ignorance and inexperience. Men saw waggons rushing hither and thither, and thought that all was lost. After that the year was passed in drilling and in camp-making, — in the making of soldiers, of gunpowder, and of cannons. But of all the articles of war made in that year, the article that seemed easiest of fabrication was a general officer. Generals were made with the greatest rapidity, owing their promotion much more frequently to local interest than to military success. Such a State sent such and such regiments, and therefore must be rewarded by having such and such generals nominated from among its citizens. The wonder perhaps is that with armies so formed battles should have been fought so well.

Before the end of 1861 both Major Reckenthorpe's sons had become general officers. That Frank, the soldier, should have been so promoted was, at such a period as this, nothing strange. Though a young man he had been a soldier, or learning the trade of a soldier, for more than ten years, and such service as that might well be counted for much in the sudden construction of an army intended to number seven hundred thousand troops, and which at one time did contain all those soldiers. Frank too was a clever fellow, who knew his business, and there were many generals made in those days who understood less of their work than he did. As much could not be said for Tom's quick military advancement. But this could be said for them in the South, — that unless they did make their generals in this way, they would hardly have any generals at all, and General Reckenthorpe, as he so quickly became, — General Tom as they used to call him in Kentucky, — recommended himself specially to the Confederate leaders by the warmth and eagerness with which he had come among them. The name of the old man so well known throughout the Union, who had ever loved the South without hating the North, would have been a tower of strength to them. Having him they would have thought that they might have carried the State of Kentucky into open secession.

He was now worn out and old, and could not be expected to take upon his shoulders the crushing burden of a new contest. But his eldest son had come among them, eagerly, with his whole heart; and so they made him a general.

The poor old man was in part proud of this and in part grieved. "I have a son a general in each army," he said to a stranger who came to his house in those days; "but what strength is there in a fagot when it is separated? of what use is a house that is divided against itself? The boys would kill each other if they met."

"It is very sad," said the stranger.

"Sad!" said the old man. "It is as though the Devil were let loose upon the earth; — and so he is; so he is."

The family came to understand that General Tom was with the Confederate army which was confronting the Federal army of the Potomac and defending Richmond; whereas it was well known that Frank was in Kentucky with the army on the Green River, which was hoping to make its way into Tennessee, and which did so early in the following year. It must be understood that Kentucky, though a slave state, had never seceded, and that therefore it was divided off from the Southern States, such as Tennessee and that part of Virginia which had seceded, by a cordon of pickets; so that there was no coming up from the Confederate army to Frankfort in Kentucky. There could, at any rate, be no easy or safe coming up for such a one as General Tom, seeing that being a soldier he would be regarded as a spy, and certainly treated as a prisoner if found within the Northern lines. Nevertheless, General as he was, he kept his engagement with Ada, and made his way into the gardens of his father's house on the night of Christmas-eve. And Ada was the first who knew that he was there. Her ear first caught the sound of his footsteps, and her hand raised for him the latch of the garden door.

"Oh, Tom, it is not you?"

"But it is though, Ada, my darling!" Then there was a little pause in his speech. "Did I not tell you that I should see you to-day?"

"Hush. Do you know who is here? Your brother came across to us from the Green River yesterday."

"The mischief he did. Then I shall never find my way back again. If you knew what I have gone through for this!"

Ada immediately stepped out through the door and on to the snow, standing close up against him as she whispered to him, "I don't think Frank would betray you," she said. "I don't think he would."

"I doubt him, — doubt him hugely. But I suppose I must trust him. I got through the pickets close to Cumberland Gap, and I left my horse at Stoneley's, halfway between this and Lexington. I cannot go back to-night now that I have come so far!"

"Wait, Tom; wait a minute, and I will go in and tell your mother. But you must be hungry. Shall I bring you food?"

"Hungry enough, but I will not eat my father's victuals out here in the snow."

"Wait a moment, dearest, till I speak to my aunt." Then Ada slipped back into the house and soon managed to get Mrs. Reckenthorpe away from the room in which the Major and his second son were sitting. "Tom is here," she said, "in the garden. He has encountered all this danger to pay us a visit because it is Christmas. Oh, aunt, what are we to do? He says that Frank would certainly give him up!"

Mrs. Reckenthorpe was nearly twenty years younger than her husband, but even with this advantage on her side Ada's tidings were almost too much for her. She, however, at last managed to consult the Major, and he resolved upon appealing to the generosity of his younger son. By this time the Confederate General was warming himself in the kitchen, having declared that his brother might do as he pleased; — he would not skulk away from his father's house in the night.

"Frank," said the father, as his younger son sat silently thinking of what had been told him, "it cannot be your duty to be false to your father in his own house."

"It is not always easy, sir, for a man to see what is his duty. I wish that either he or I had not come here."

"But he is here; and you, his brother, would not take

seen Ada Forster since that former Christmas when they had all been together, and he had now left his camp and come across from the army much more with the view of inducing her to acknowledge the hopelessness of her engagement with his brother, than from any domestic idea of passing his Christmas at home. He was a man who would not have interfered with his brother's prospects, as regarded either love or money, if he had thought that in doing so he would in truth have injured his brother. He was a hard man, but one not wilfully unjust. He had satisfied himself that a marriage between Ada and his brother must, if it were practicable, be ruinous to both of them. If this were so, would not it be better for all parties that there should be another arrangement made? North and South were as far divided now as the two poles. All Ada's hopes and feelings were with the North. Could he allow her to be taken as a bride among perishing slaves and ruined whites?

But when the moment for his sudden departure came he knew that it would be better that he should go without seeing her. His brother Tom had made his way to her through cold, and wet, and hunger, and through infinite perils of a kind sterner even than these. Her heart now would be full of softness towards him. So Frank Reckenthorpe left the house without seeing any one but his mother. Ada, as the front door closed behind him, was still standing close by her lover

over the kitchen fire, while the slaves of the family, with whom Master Tom had always been the favourite, were administering to his little comforts.

Of course General Tom was a hero in the house for the few days that he remained there, and of course the step he had taken was the very one to strengthen for him the affection of the girl whom he had come to see. North and South were even more bitterly divided now than they had been when the former parting had taken place. There were fewer hopes of reconciliation; more positive certainty of war to the knife; and they who adhered strongly to either side, and those who did not adhere strongly to either side were very few, — held their opinions now with more acrimony than they had then done. The peculiar bitterness of civil war, which adds personal hatred to national enmity, had come upon the minds of the people. And here, in Kentucky, on the borders of the contest, members of the same household were, in many cases, at war with each other. Ada Forster and her aunt were passionately Northern, while the feelings of the old man had gradually turned themselves to that division in the nation to which he naturally belonged. For months past the matter on which they were all thinking, — the subject which filled their minds morning, noon, and night, — was banished from their lips because it could not be discussed without the bitterness of hostility. But, nevertheless, there was no word of bitterness between Tom Reckenthorpe and Ada Forster. While these few short days lasted it was all love. Where is the woman whom one touch of romance will not soften, though she be ever so impervious to argument? Tom could sit upstairs with his mother and his betrothed, and tell them stories of the gallantry of the South, — of the sacrifices women were making, and of the deeds men were doing, — and they would listen and smile and caress his hand, and all for a while would be pleasant; while the old Major did not dare to speak before them of his Southern hopes. But down in the parlour, during the two or three long nights which General Tom passed in Frankfort, open secession was discussed between the two men. The old man now had given away altogether. The Yankees, he said, were too bitter for him. "I wish I had died first; that is all," he said. "I wish I had died first. Life is wretched now to a man who can do nothing." His son tried to comfort him, saying that secession would certainly be accomplished in twelve months, and that every Slave State would certainly be included in the Southern Confederacy. But the Major shook his head. Though he hated the political bitterness of the men whom he called Puritans and Yankees, he knew their strength and acknowledged their power. "Nothing good can come in my time," he said; "not in my time, — not in my time."

In the middle of the fourth night General Tom took his departure. An old slave arrived with his horse a little before midnight, and he started on his journey. "Whatever turns up, Ada," he said, "you will be true to me."

"I will; though you are a rebel, all the same for that."

"So was Washington."

"Washington made a nation; — you are destroying one."

"We are making another, dear; that's all. But I won't talk secesh to you out here in the cold. Go in, and be good to my father; and remember this, Ada, I'll be here again next Christmas-eve, if I'm alive."

So he went, and made his journey back to his camp in safety. He slept at a friend's house during the following day, and on the next night again made his way through the Northern lines back into Virginia. Even at that time there was considerable danger in doing this, although the frontier to be guarded was so extensive. This arose chiefly from the paucity of roads, and the impossibility of getting across the country where no roads existed. But General Tom got safely back to Richmond, and no doubt found that the tedium of his military life had been greatly relieved by his excursion.

Then, after that, came a year of fighting, — and there has since come another year of fighting; of such fighting that we, hearing the accounts from day to day, have hitherto failed to recognise its extent and import. Every now and then we have even spoken of the inaction of this side or of that, as though the drawn battles which have lasted for days, in which men have perished by tens of thousands, could be renewed as might the old German battles, in which an Austrian general would be ever retreating with infinite skill and military efficacy. For constancy, for blood, for hard determination to win at any cost of life or material, history has known no such battles as these. That the South has fought the best as regards skill no man can doubt. As regards pluck and resolution there has not been a pin's choice between them. They have both fought as Englishmen fight when they are equally in earnest. As regards result, it has been almost altogether in favour of the North, because they have so vast a superiority in numbers and material.

General Tom Reckenthorpe remained during the year in Virginia, and was attached to that corps of General Lee's army which was commanded by Stonewall Jackson. It was not probable, therefore, that he would be left without active employment. During the whole year he was fighting, assisting in the wonderful raids that were made by that man whose loss was worse to the Confederates than the loss of Vicksburg or of New Orleans. And General Tom gained for himself mark, name, and glory, — but it was the glory of a soldier rather than of a general. No one looked upon him as the future commander of an army; but men said that if there was a rapid stroke to be stricken, under orders from some more thoughtful head, General Tom was the hand to strike it. Thus he went on making wonderful rides by night, appearing like a warrior ghost leading warrior ghosts in some quiet valley of the Federals, seizing supplies and cutting off cattle, till his name came to be great in the State of Kentucky, and Ada Forster, Yankee though she was, was proud of her rebel lover.

And Frank Reckenthorpe, the other general, made progress also, though it was progress of a different kind. Men did not talk of him so much as they did of Tom; but the War Office at Washington knew that he was useful, — and used him. He remained for a long time attached to the western army, having been removed from Kentucky to St. Louis, in Missouri, and was there when his brother last heard of him. "I am fighting day and night," he once said to one who was with him from his own State, "and, as far as I can learn, Frank is writing day and night. Upon my word, I think that I have the best of it."

It was but a couple of days after this, the time then being about the latter end of September, that he found himself on horseback at the head of three regiments of cavalry near the foot of one of those valleys which lead up into the Blue Mountain ridge of Virginia. He was about six miles in advance of Jackson's army, and had pushed forward with the view of intercepting certain Federal supplies which he and others had hoped might be within his reach. He had expected that there would be fighting, but he had hardly expected so much fighting as came that day in his way. He got no supplies. Indeed, he got nothing but blows, and though on that day the Confederates would not admit that they had been worsted, neither could they claim to have done more than hold their own. But General Tom's fighting was in that day brought to an end.

It must be understood that there was no great battle fought on this occasion. General Reckenthorpe, with about 1500 troopers, had found himself suddenly compelled to attack about double that number of Federal infantry. He did so once, and then a second time, but on each occasion without breaking the lines to which he was opposed; and towards the close of the day he found himself unhorsed, but still unwounded, with no weapon in his hand but his pistol, immediately surrounded by about a dozen of his own men, but so far in advance of the body of his troops as to make it almost impossible that he should find his way back to them. As the smoke cleared away and he could look about him, he saw that he was close to an uneven, irregular line of Federal soldiers. But there was still a chance, and he had turned for a rush, with his pistol ready for use in his hand, when he found himself confronted by a Federal officer. The pistol was already raised, and his finger was on the trigger, when he saw that the man before him was his brother.

"Your time has come," said Frank, standing his ground very calmly. He was quite unarmed, and had been separated from his men and ridden over; but hitherto he had not been hurt.

"Frank!" said Tom, dropping his pistol arm, "is that you?"

"And you are not going to do it, then?" said Frank.

"Do what?" said Tom, whose calmness was altogether gone. But he had forgotten that threat as soon as it had been uttered, and did not even know to what his brother was alluding.

But Tom Reckenthorpe, in his confusion at meeting his brother, had lost whatever chance there remained to him of escaping. He stood for a moment or two, looking at Frank, and wondering at the coincidence which had brought them together, before he turned to run. Then it was too late. In the hurry and scurry of the affair all but two of his own men had left him, and he saw that a rush of Federal soldiers was coming up around him. Nevertheless he resolved to start for a run. "Give me a chance, Frank," he said, and prepared to run. But as he went, — or rather before he had left the ground on which he was standing before his brother, a shot struck him, and he was disabled. In a minute he was as though he were stunned; then he smiled faintly, and slowly sunk upon the ground. "It's all up, Frank," he said, "and you are in at the death."

Frank Reckenthorpe was soon kneeling beside his brother amidst a crowd of his own men. "Spurrell," he said to a young officer who was close to him, "it is my own brother." — "What, General Tom?" said Spurrell. "Not dangerously, I hope?"

By this time the wounded man had been able, as it were, to feel himself and to ascertain the amount of the damage done him. "It's my right leg," he said; "just on the knee. If you'll believe me, Frank, I thought it was my heart at first. I don't think much of the wound, but I suppose you won't let me go?"

Of course they wouldn't let him go, and indeed if they had been minded so to do, he could not have gone. The wound was not fatal, as he had at first thought; but neither was it a matter of little consequence as he afterwards asserted. His fighting was over, unless he could fight with a leg amputated between the knee and the hip.

Before nightfall General Tom found himself in his brother's quarters, a prisoner on parole, with his leg all but condemned by the surgeon. The third day after that saw the leg amputated. For three weeks the two brothers remained together, and after that the elder was taken to

Washington, — or rather to Alexandria, on the other side of the Potomac, as a prisoner, there to wait his chance of exchange. At first the intercourse between the two brothers was cold, guarded, and uncomfortable; but after a while it became more kindly than it had been for many a day. Whether it were cold or kindly, its nature, we may be sure, was such as the younger brother made it. Tom was ready enough to forget all personal animosity as soon as his brother would himself be willing to do so; though he was willing enough also to quarrel, — to quarrel bitterly as ever, — if Frank should give him occassion. As to that threat of the pistol, it had passed away from Tom Reckenthorpe, as all his angry words passed from him. It was clean forgotten. It was not simply that he had not wished to kill his brother, but that such a deed was impossible to him. The threat had been like a curse that means nothing, — which is used by passion as its readiest weapon when passion is impotent. But with Frank Reckenthorpe words meant what they were intended to mean. The threat had rankled in his bosom from the time of its utterance, to that moment when a strange coincidence had given the threatener the power of executing it. The remembrance of it was then strong upon him, and he had expected that his brother would have been as bad as his word. But his brother had spared him; and now, slowly, by degrees, he began to remember that also.

"What are your plans, Tom?" he said, as he sat one day by his brother's bed before the removal of the prisoner to Alexandria.

"Plans," said Tom. "How should a poor fellow like me have plans? To eat bread and water in prison at Alexandria, I suppose."

"They'll let you up to Washington on your parole, I should think. Of course I can say a word for you."

"Well, then, do say it. I'd have done as much for you, though I don't like your Yankee politics."

"Never mind my politics now, Tom."

"I never did mind them. But at any rate, you see I can't run away."

It should have been mentioned a little way back in this story that the poor old Major had been gathered to his fathers during the past year. As he had said to himself, it would be better for him that he should die. He had lived to see the glory of his country, and had gloried in it. If further glory or even further gain were to come out of this terrible war, — as great gains to men and nations do come from contests which are very terrible while they last, — he at least would not live to see it. So when he was left by his sons, he turned his face to the wall and died. There had of course been much said on this subject between the two brothers when they were together, and Frank had declared how special orders had been given to protect the house of the widow if the waves of the war in Kentucky should surge up around Frankfort. Land very near to Frankfort had become debatable between the two armies, and the question of flying from their house had more than once been mooted between the aunt and her niece; but, so far, that evil day had been staved off, and as yet Frankfort, the little capital of the State, was Northern territory.

"I suppose you will get home?" said Frank, after musing awhile, "and look after my mother and Ada?"

"If I can I shall, of course. What else can I do with one leg?"

"Nothing in this war, Tom, of course." Then there was another pause between them. "And what will Ada do?" said Frank.

"What will Ada do? Stay at home with my mother."

"Ah, — yes. But she will not remain always as Ada Forster."

"Do you mean to ask whether I shall marry her; — because of my one leg? If she will have me, I certainly shall."

"And will she? Ought you to ask her?"

"If I found her seamed all over with small-pox, with her limbs broken, blind, disfigured by any misfortune which could have visited her, I would take her as my wife all the same. If she were pennyless it would make no difference. She shall judge for herself; but I shall expect her to act by me, as I would have acted by her." Then there was another pause. "Look here, Frank," continued General Tom; "if you mean that I am to give her up as a reward to you for being sent home, I will have nothing to do with the bargain."

"I had intended no such bargain," said Frank, gloomily.

"Very well; then you can do as you please. If Ada will take me, I shall marry her as soon as she will let me. If my being sent home depends upon that, you will know how to act now."

Nevertheless he was sent home. There was not another word spoken between the two brothers about Ada Forster. Whether Frank thought that he might still have a chance through want of firmness on the part of the girl; or whether he considered that in keeping his brother away from home he could at least do himself no good; or whether, again, he resolved that he would act by his brother as a brother should act, without reference to Ada Forster, I will not attempt to say. For a day or two after the above conversation he was somewhat sullen, and did not talk freely with his brother. After that he brightened up once more, and before long the two parted on friendly terms. General Frank remained with his command, and General Tom was sent to the hospital at Alexandria, — or to such hospitalities as he might be able to enjoy at Washington in his mutilated state, — till that affair of his exchange had been arranged.

In spite of his brother's influence at headquarters this could not be done in a day; nor could permission be obtained for him to go home to Kentucky till such exchange had been effected. In this way he was kept in terrible suspense for something over two months, and mid-winter was upon him before the joyful news arrived that he was free to go where he liked. The officials in Washington would have sent him back to Richmond had he so pleased, seeing that a Federal general officer, supposed to be of equal weight with himself, had been sent back from some Southern prison in his place; but he declined any such favour, declaring his intention of going home to Kentucky. He was simply warned that no pass South could after this be granted to him, and then he went his way.

Disturbed as was the state of the country, nevertheless railways ran from Washington to Baltimore, from Baltimore to Pittsburgh, from Pittsburgh to Cincinnati, and from Cincinnati to Frankfort. So that General Tom's journey home, though with but one leg, was made much faster, and with less difficulty, than that last journey by which he reached the old family house. And again he presented himself on Christmas-eve. Ada declared that he remained purposely at

Washington, so that he might make good his last promise to the letter; but I am inclined to think that he allowed no such romantic idea as that to detain him among the amenities of Washington.

He arrived again after dark, but on this occasion did not come knocking at the back door. He had fought his fight, had done his share of the battle, and now had reason to be afraid of no one. But again it was Ada who opened the door for him. "Oh, Tom; oh, my own one." There never was a word of question between them as to whether that unseemly crutch and still unhealed wound was to make any difference between them. General Tom found before three hours were over that he lacked the courage to suggest that he might not be acceptable to her as a lover with one leg. There are times in which girls throw off all their coyness, and are as bold in their loves as men. Such a time was this with Ada Forster. In the course of another month the elder General simply sent word to the younger that they intended to be married in May, if the war did not prevent them; and the younger General simply sent back word that his duties at headquarters would prevent his being present at the ceremony.

And they were married in May, though the din of war was going on around them on every side. And from that time to this the din of war is still going on, and they are in the thick of it. The carnage of their battles, the hatreds of their civil contests, are terrible to us when we think of them; but may it not be that the beneficient power of Heaven, which they acknowledge as we do, is thus cleansing their land from that stain of slavery, to abolish which no human power seemed to be sufficient?

# Not If I Know It

OT IF I KNOW IT." IT WAS AN ILL-NATURED answer to give, made in the tone that was used, by a brother-in-law to a brother-in-law, in the hearing of the sister of the one and wife of the other, — made, too, on Christmas Eve, when the married couple had come as visitors to the house of him who made it! There was no joke in the words, and the man who had uttered them had gone for the night. There was to be no other farewell spoken indicative of the brightness of the coming day. "Not if I know it!" and the door was slammed behind him. The words were very harsh in the ears even of a loving sister.

"He was always a cur," said the husband.

"No; not so. George has his ill-humours and his little periods of bad temper; but he was not always a cur. Don't say so of him, Wilfred."

"He always was so to me. He wanted you to marry that fellow Cross because he had a lot of money."

"But I didn't," said the wife, who now had been three years married to Wilfred Horton.

"I cannot understand that you and he should have been children of the same parents. Just the use of his name, and there would be no risk."

"I suppose he thinks that there might have been risk," said the wife. "He cannot know you as I do."

"Had he asked me I would have given him mine without thinking of it. Though he knows that I am a busy man, I have never asked him to lend me a shilling. I never will."

"Wilfred!"

"All right, old girl — I am going to bed; and you will see that I shall treat him to-morrow just as though he had refused me nothing. But I shall think that he is a cur." And Wilfred Horton prepared to leave the room.

"Wilfred!"

"Well, Mary, out with it."

"Curs are curs —— "

"Because other curs make them so; that is what you are going to say."

"No, dear, no; I will never call you a cur, because I know well that you are not one. There is nothing like a cur about you." Then she took him in her arms and kissed him. "But if there be any signs of ill-humour in a man, the way to in-crease it is to think much of it. Men are curs because other men think them so; women are angels sometimes, just be-cause some loving husband like you tells them that they are. How can a woman not have something good about her when everything she does is taken to be good? I could be as cross as George is if only I were called cross. I don't suppose you want the use of his name so very badly."

"But I have condescended to ask for it. And then to be answered with that jeering pride! I wouldn't have his name to a paper now, though you and I were starving for the want of it. As it is, it doesn't much signify. I suppose you won't be long before you come." So saying, he took his departure.

She followed him, and went through the house till she came to her brother's apartments. He was a bachelor, and was living all alone when he was in the country at Hallam Hall. It was a large, rambling house, in which there had been of custom many visitors at Christmas time. But Mrs. Wade, the widow, had died during the past year, and there was nobody there now but the owner of the house, and his sister, and his sister's husband. She followed him to his rooms, and found him sitting alone, with a pipe in his mouth, and as she entered she saw that preparations had been made for the comfort of more than one person. "If there be any-thing that I hate," said George Wade, "it is to be asked for the use of my name. I would sooner lend money to a fellow at once, — or give it to him."

"There is no question about money, George."

"Oh, isn't there? I never knew a man's name wanted when there was no question about money."

"I suppose there is a question — in some remote degree." Here George Wade shook his head. "In some remote degree," she went on repeating her words. "Surely you know him well enough not to be afraid of him."

"I know no man well enough not to be afraid of him where my name is concerned."

"You need not have refused him so crossly, just on Christmas Eve."

"I don't know much about Christmas where money is wanted."

"'Not if I know it!' you said."

"I simply meant that I did not wish to do it. Wilfred expects that everybody should answer him with such constrained courtesy! What I said was as good a way of answering him as any other; and if he didn't like it — he must lump it."

"Is that the message that you send him?" she asked.

"I don't send it as a message at all. If he wants a message you may tell him that I'm extremely sorry, but that it's against my principles. You are not going to quarrel with me as well as he?"

"Indeed, no," she said, as she prepared to leave him for the night. "I should be very unhappy to quarrel with either of you." Then she went.

"He is the most punctilious fellow living at this moment, I believe," said George Wade, as he walked alone up and down the room. There were certain regrets which did make the moment bitter to him. His brother-in-law had on the whole treated him well, — had been liberal to him in all those matters in which one brother comes in contact with another. He had never asked him for a shilling, or even for the use of his name. His sister was passionately devoted to her husband. In fact, he knew Wilfred Horton to be a fine fellow. He told himself that he had not meant to be especially uncourteous, but that he had been at the moment startled by the expression of Horton's wishes. But looking back over his own conduct, he could remember that in the course of their intimacy he himself had been occasionally rough to his brother-in-law, and he could remember that his brother-in-law had not liked it. "After all what does it mean, 'Not if I know it'? It is just a form of saying that I had rather not." Nevertheless, Wilfred Horton could not persuade himself to go to bed in a good humour with George Wade.

"I think I shall get back to London to-morrow," said Mr. Horton, speaking to his wife from beneath the bedclothes, as soon as she had entered the room.

"To-morrow?"

"It is not that I cannot bear his insolence, but that I should have to show by my face that I had made a request, and had been refused. You need not come."

"On Christmas Day?"

"Well, yes. You cannot understand the sort of flutter I am in. 'Not if I know it!' The insolence of the phrase in answering such a request! The suspicion that it showed! If he had told me that he had any feeling about it, I would have deposited the money in his hands. There is a train in the morning. You can stay here and go to church with him, while I run up to town."

"That you two should part like that on Christmas Day; you two dear ones! Wilfred, it will break my heart." Then he turned round and endeavoured to make himself comfortable among the bedclothes. "Wilfred, say that you will not go out of this to-morrow."

"Oh, very well! You have only to speak and I obey. If you could only manage to make your brother more civil for the one day it would be an improvement."

"I think he will be civil. I have been speaking to him, and he seems to be sorry that he should have annoyed you."

"Well, yes; he did annoy me. 'Not if I know it!' in answer to such a request! As if I had asked him for five thousand pounds! I wouldn't have asked him or any man alive for five thousand pence. Coming down to his house at Christmas-time, and to be suspected of such a thing!" Then he prepared himself steadily to sleep, and she, before she stretched herself by his side, prayed that God's mercy might obliterate the wrath between these men, whom she loved so well, before the morrow's sun should have come and gone.

The bells sounded merry from Hallam Church tower on the following morning, and told to each of the inhabitants of the old hall a tale that was varied according to the minds of the three inhabitants whom we know. With her it was all hope, but hope accompanied by that despondency which is apt to afflict the weak in the presence of those that are stronger. With her husband it was anger, — but mitigated anger. He seemed, as he came into his wife's room while dressing, to be aware that there was something which should be abandoned, but which still it did his heart some good to nourish. With George Wade there was more of Christian feeling, but of Christian feeling which it was disagreeable to entertain. "How on earth is a man to get on with his relatives, if he cannot speak a word above his breath?" But still he would have been very willing that those words should have been left unsaid.

Any observer might have seen that the three persons as they sat down to breakfast were each under some little constraint. The lady was more than ordinarily courteous, or even affectionate, in her manner. This was natural on Christmas Day, but her too apparent anxiety was hardly natural. Her husband accosted his brother-in-law with almost loud good humour. "Well, George, a merry Christmas, and many of them. My word; — how hard it froze last night! You won't get any hunting for the next fortnight. I hope old Burnaby won't spin us a long yarn."

George Wade simply kissed his sister, and shook hands with his brother-in-law. But he shook hands with more apparent zeal than he would have done but for the quarrel, and when he pressed Wilfred Horton to eat some devilled turkey, he did it with more ardour than was usual with him. "Mrs. Jones is generally very successful with devilled turkey." Then, as he passed round the table behind his sister's back, she put out her hand to touch him, and as though to thank him for his goodness. But any one could see that it was not quite natural.

The two men as they left the house for church, were thinking of the request that had been made yesterday, and which had been refused. "Not if I know it!" said George Wade to himself. "There is nothing so unnatural in that, that a fellow should think so much of it. I didn't mean to do it. Of course, if he had said that he wanted it particularly I should have done it."

"Not if I know it!" said Wilfred Horton. "There was an

insolence about it. I only came to him just because he was my brother-in-law. Jones, or Smith, or Walker would have done it without a word." Then the three walked into church, and took their places in the front seat, just under Dr. Burnaby's reading-desk.

We will not attempt to describe the minds of the three as the Psalms were sung, and as the prayers were said. A twinge did cross the minds of the two men as the coming of the Prince of Peace was foretold to them; and a stronger hope did sink into the heart of her whose happiness depended so much on the manner in which they two stood with one another. And when Dr. Burnaby found time, in the fifteen minutes which he gave to his sermon, to tell his hearers why the Prophet had specially spoken of Christ as the Prince of Peace, and to describe what the blessings were, hitherto unknown, which had come upon the world since a desire for peace had filled the minds of men, a feeling did come on the hearts of both of them, — to one that the words had better not have been spoken, and to the other that they had better have been forgiven. Then came the Sacrament, more powerful with its thoughts than its words, and the two men as they left the church were ready to forgive each other — if they only knew how.

There was something a little sheep-faced about the two men as they walked up together across the grounds to the old hall, — something sheep-faced which Mrs. Horton fully understood, and which made her feel for the moment triumphant over them. It is always so with a woman when she knows that she has for the moment got the better of a man. How much more so when she has conquered two? She hovered about among them as though they were dear human beings subject to the power of some beneficent angel. The three sat down to lunch, and Dr. Burnaby could not but have been gratified had he heard the things that were said of him. "I tell you, you know," said George, "that Burnaby is a right good fellow, and awfully clever. There isn't a man or woman in the parish that he doesn't know how to get to the inside of."

"And he knows what to do when he gets there," said Mrs. Horton, who remembered with affection the gracious old parson as he had blessed her at her wedding.

"No; I couldn't let him do it for me." It was thus Horton spoke to his wife as they were walking together about the gardens. "Dear Wilfred, you ought to forgive him."

"I have forgiven him. There!" And he made a sign as of blowing his anger away to the winds. "I do forgive him. I will think no more about it. It is as though the words had never been spoken, — though they were very unkind. 'Not if I know it!' All the same, they don't leave a sting behind."

"But they do."

"Nothing of the kind. I shall drink prosperity to the old

house and a loving wife to the master just as cheerily by and by as though the words had never been spoken."

"But there will not be peace, — not the peace of which Dr. Burnaby told us. It must be as though it had really — really never been uttered. George has not spoken to me about it, not to-day, but if he asks, you will let him do it?"

"He will never ask — unless at your instigation."

"I will not speak to him," she answered, — "not without telling you. I would never go behind your back. But whether he does it or not, I feel that it is in his heart to do it." Then the brother came up and joined them in their walk, and told them of all the little plans he had in hand in reference to the garden. "You must wait till *she* comes, for that, George," said his sister.

"Oh, yes; there must always be a she when another she is talking. But what will you say if I tell you there is to be a she?"

"Oh, George!"

"Your nose is going to be put out of joint, as far as Hallam Hall is concerned." Then he told them all his love story, and so the afternoon was allowed to wear itself away till the dinner hour had nearly come.

"Just come in here, Wilfred," he said to his brother-in-law when his sister had gone up to dress. "I have something I want to say to you before dinner."

"All right," said Wilfred. And as he got up to follow the master of the house, he told himself that after all his wife would prove herself too many for him.

"I don't know the least in the world what it was you were asking me to do yesterday."

"It was a matter of no consequence," said Wilfred, not able to avoid assuming an air of renewed injury.

"But I do know that I was cross," said George Wade.

"After that," said Wilfred, "everything is smooth between us. No man can expect anything more straightforward. I was a little hurt, but I know that I was a fool. Every man has a right to have his own ideas as to the use of his name."

"But that will not suffice," said George.

"Oh! yes it will."

"Not for me," repeated George. "I have brought myself to ask your pardon for refusing, and you should bring yourself to accept my offer to do it."

"It was nothing. It was only because you were my brother-in-law, and therefore the nearest to me. The Turco-Egyptian New Waterworks Company simply requires somebody to assert that I am worth ten thousands pounds."

"Let me do it, Wilfred," said George Wade. "Nobody can know your circumstances better than I do. I have begged your pardon, and I think that you ought now in return to accept this at my hand."

"All right," said Wilfred Horton. "I will accept it at your hand." And then he went away to dress. What took place up in the dressing-room need not here be told. But when Mrs. Horton came down to dinner the smile upon her face was a truer index of her heart than it had been in the morning.

"I have been very sorry for what took place last night," said George afterwards in the drawing-room, feeling himself obliged, as it were, to make full confession and restitution before the assembled multitude, — which consisted, however, of his brother-in-law and his sister. "I have asked pardon, and have begged Wilfred to show his grace by accepting from me what I had before declined. I hope that he will not refuse me."

"Not if I know it," said Wilfred Horton.